The Scheme

By

Ash Thakur

Contents

Chapter 1

Someone must have spoken highly of Julian Kay – he had always kept a low profile – because early one morning he got a visit from two people who were very eager to meet him. He hadn't yet drunk his first cup of Earl Grey (*always* with milk) when he heard the loud, impatient knocking on his front door. His girlfriend Stephanie, who habitually woke up ten minutes before him, sometimes brought him his tea while he propped himself up on his pillows. But not today; so, he got up to retrieve it from the worktop next to the kettle, firm on his feet despite last night's entertaining. He felt grateful that he had lately become a stick-to-the-two-glasses drinker. God knows, he needed to be these days.

The knocking grew louder and more forceful, but then stopped dead leaving an eerie silence. Then, a man's voice, not quite as confident as the percussion that had announced it: "Hello? *Hi!* Hope you don't mind, but..."

Julian snorted his morning snort, inhaled deeply and took a big slurp of hot fragrant liquid from the mug in his hand. He was wearing his new and expensive dark blue silk dressing gown. Cocking his head back slightly, he swung open the front door. There stood a man in his late fifties, accompanied by a woman of a similar age.

"I did ring the bell, but–" Julian shifted his weight onto his back foot and they saw their chance to dart inside. "We're *so* sorry to drop in on you like this!" said the man.

"Not at all." Julian put on his half welcoming, half interested expression. "Tell me, what can I do for you?"

"Look, sorry. Let me start by introducing myself. I'm Paul Kelmer. Your father in law, Clive – well, I'm his accountant. You may have heard my name mentioned?"

"Ah yes. Well it's nice to put a name to a face." Paul's face was large, square and friendly with strong, not particularly regular features. A bristly, greying moustache helped to offset them. "No father in law yet, but I must say Clive does his best. Stephanie's my fiancée, actually." A slim blonde figure scampered from the kitchen to the living room, and Paul's eyes followed her for a second. Without stopping she glanced at him and smiled.

Paul continued, "We're actually off on our hols today. Flying out to the house in Alicante this afternoon. Hence the rush! You know, Louisa and I have heard *all about* what you've been doing, everything you've achieved so far, and I must say, I think it's really quite brilliant. You young chaps… " – he looked a little sheepish – "you know, I've been in this business, in the *financial* business for yonks now, but never really figured out how the markets work. It just all seems like gambling to me. By the way, you've got a beautiful house!" Louisa nodded vigorously, whilst her perfect ash blonde and grey (no mauve yet) hairdo remained static.

Julian, who had been standing motionless, still on his back foot, looked down at the cherrywood floor (his choice), then up at the cream and claret colour scheme for the ceiling and walls (Stephanie's). "Thank you. Most of it is Steph's work."

"So – what's the minimum investment? We want in, as you've probably guessed by now. But being an accountant I tend to be cautious. My clients pay me for it, ha ha. So how about we go in really lowball, starting off with say, twenty-five grand? Is that okay for starters?" Louisa helpfully confirmed that they always like to be on the safe side.

"Sure," said Julian. "I don't see why not. Any lower than that and you start getting problems with administration costs, broker's fees and such like but yeah, we could get going with that."

Paul began to stab the air with his index finger. "But mark my words Julian, there'll be more on the way, and I mean a *lot* more, once we see some initial results. What is it you do exactly? Foreign currencies?"

Julian had some impressive sounding 'technical' vocabulary to fend off questions. "FX volatility arbitrage.

You see, when the markets are particularly active, you've got standard deviations–"

Even Julian was surprised by how effectively it had worked. Paul held up his hand and waved it slowly, his eyes rolling. "Look, don't bother going into details. It's too early, and I'm too old. I trust you, and I must say, the profits look terrific. What's the catch? Is there one? Probably ninety-nine percent income tax or something, ha ha. But about those returns: they're definitely between three and five percent per month, right? Or so I understand?"

Julian frowned slightly and made the 'shhh' shape with his lips. "That's correct."

Paul continued in a softer voice: "So, just to clarify: the three percent – that's per *month* – that's guaranteed, right? And the other two percent, which could take it up to five percent – once again, per month – that depends on whatever the actual currencies have been doing, right?"

"Yes. Correct. That's the way it's been working so far, certainly."

"Okay!" He and Louisa beamed at each other. "Here's my card. The email address is just at the bottom there. Can I count on you to send me all the forms and related paperwork? We've got plenty of time to complete everything while we're in Spain. While we're lounging by the pool, right Louisa?"

"Lucky you! But Paul, just one thing. I'd prefer to keep this to friends and family only, at least for the time being. You know, when something's doing really well you don't want to attract the wrong sort of attention. Some people can be very negative, sadly."

"Understood!" Paul grinned with the force and finality normally provided by a firm handshake. As he shut the front gate on their way out, he smiled, looked back and shouted, "Dad in law should be very proud of you."

Julian was tempted to go back to bed with his tea, but then remembered that such an early morning mention of his father-in-law-to-be had served as a warning. He recalled a childhood ditty, something about shepherds and red sky in the morning. "Steph!" he called, turning in the direction of the kitchen, "What time are your folks coming round?"

"Midday. Or just after," came her voice from the living room, "It's sort of an early lunch. But not quite brunch. They'll expect proper food, I'm sure."

Julian walked into the living room. Stephanie was lying back on the sofa with her bare legs, crossed at the ankles, resting on the coffee table. He noticed that she had painted her toenails a very dark shade of maroon. "Are you planning on cooking?"

She flexed her toes. "Sure. Goat curry. I'm actually using lamb, it's just that it's *called* goat curry."

"So that's what they teach you at cookery school?"

"Among other things." She smiled coquettishly. "The funny thing is you think I go there to learn how to cook. I already can *cook*. Didn't I tell you our instructor is seriously sexy?"

"Yes, thrice now. Listen, Steph – I have to pop out for a while. I'll be back in no time, way before noon."

"A real quickie then? Ok, see you soon, with your mouth watering for my goat. It's going to be spicy, the way you like it."

The Kays' north London suburb was often described by estate agents as a village, although Julian thought just about anywhere in London not overlooking a dual carriageway could be described thus. It had enough of the spacious greenness that gives one a sense of calm and really having left the centre of town whilst retaining some interesting Victorian and Regency red brick architecture. Normal middle class people, those skilled, numerate professionals who toil in open plan offices and consider a seat on a tube train a blessing had long since lost the ability to purchase a house here. A cramped apartment was the best most of them could aim for, the financial burden to be further eased by the practice of flat sharing. Julian thought maybe once in a while that could lead to a lifelong friendship.

He walked the familiar route to up to his favourite café on the narrow, winding high street. He walked briskly and easily, having shed the last remnants of childhood asthma years ago. Unencumbered by briefcase, laptop or umbrella – it was a lovely early Summer morning, too – he reflected on how others might see him. As a lucky chap, a guy who had landed on his feet, perhaps? Or someone of exceptional ability? He knew that the reality for most Londoners was struggling to pay the bills at the end of each month; a month spent quietly hating their boss.

Café Franz was dark, dingy, comfortable and familiar; in short, perfect. What was remarkable was that the furnishings had remained unchanged in appearance from the late nineteen seventies: its teak effect formica tables, oversized sponge stuffed orange seating and swirly brown carpet were actually being imitated elsewhere in the capital. The second generation of the Italian family that had taken over from the original Austrian Jewish founder knew perfectly well that the well-heeled locals would howl if any attempt were made to 'modernise'. The food lived up to the décor, with beans on toast being the most ordered dish (by Julian at any rate). All that had changed was, possibly, the increased use of rapeseed oil.

Julian filled his nostrils with the soothing musty smell of the cafe and sat down in the corner. He had no papers or laptop with him. Nothing remotely A4 sized. No, that's just far too risky; anyone can look over your shoulder. What he did have was a mini smartphone, something quite ancient by technology standards: it was about five years old. Squinting at the tiny, brightly glowing screen he pulled up a file. Or more accurately, *the* file. The one that contained everything that had got him this far in life, from cherrywood floors to the fascinating girl who walked barefoot on them. The success file.

The file had four columns: Name, Occupation, Starting Balance, and – the really important one – Theoretical Balance. That was essentially what the investor thought he had in his account. Put simply it was equal to the starting balance (which was real enough:

basically, the cash an investor had stumped up to buy in) plus any investment "growth", minus all the cash amounts that the investor had taken out. That last bit was tricky. Any good investment advisor will tell his eager customer not to cash in the profit he's just made but to keep it working for him, keep it growing. Withdrawals can be supremely irritating, not to mention harmful; but when people insist, what can you do? In the best tradition of gentleman fraudsters and well-dressed persuaders, Julian was a man who always stayed calm.

'High yield' investment scheme lesson number one: new customers' money is used to pay 'profits' to existing customers. Lesson number two: obviously, you have to keep finding new customers. There isn't really a lesson three other than that number two will keep you *very* busy. And Julian had always been prepared to work hard.

He added "Paul Kelmer, £25,000" in blue text – black was reserved for funds that had cleared – and emailed him the signing up forms. That would normally have been that, but this time he began scrolling up and down the file to remind himself of the punters he had signed up so far. Fragments of lives, personalities and finances played with his memory.

There was Sunil Sharma, his dentist, successful and intensely practical. He spent his days shuttling between his swish practice in North London and its mirror image clone south of the river. A busy man of many projects, he had pondered Julian's investment proposition briefly and then replied with "Yeah, let's go for it. I'll put in a hundred grand. This is going to be a cash cow". Every six months Julian returned for his check-up. Neither the man nor his dentist spoke a word about money, but instead discussed every other topic beloved of innocent people. As they chatted, both men glowed with the knowledge that impressive wealth was being created while Julian's teeth were getting serviced.

And also George McCrum, his neighbour three doors away, an elderly, straight talking man known locally as "the inventor". He held a patent on some sort of gas valve and had apparently done very well out of it. He had been the hardest to persuade. A mathematician and scientist by training, he had genuinely wanted to understand exactly how Julian was generating such huge profits. The quizzing had become intense. On the verge of being caught out, Julian had got up to leave, with the parting words: "Well, look, perhaps it's not for you. Not everyone can adopt a new mindset." A firm grey hand on his shoulder as he got to the door had ensured he wouldn't be leaving without a hefty chunk of McCrum's money: "You mark my words, sunshine. Old McCrum doesn't miss out on profit!"

His favourite was Marek Wybrowsky, a builder. He had redecorated the Kays' house the previous year and nowadays was to be found hard at work in the surrounding streets, thriving on referrals and the relentless rise in property prices. A consistently cheerful young man with a balding head, huge shoulders and a paunch nurtured on gallons of imported Polish lager, he and his girlfriend Maria had struggled to come up with their ten thousand pounds starting investment (Julian had let them in with less than the usual twenty-five thousand pound minimum). They had certainly been enjoying the results. Maria's shoe collection and Marek's wardrobe of jeans and leather jackets had been moving upmarket in recent months. The belly was growing too, slowly but reassuringly.

Julian basked momentarily in the warm feeling that he was making people happy, improving their lives and fulfilling dreams. But it occurred to him that virtually nothing had changed about his own life. Visibly, at any rate. True, he had bought a bigger house, but that was really Stephanie's project. He still drove the same car and wore the same chain store suits, ate at cheap cafes and drank at old men's pubs with proper beer. But he felt the change inside. Life seemed to have more edge, that delicious danger that, he believed, a certain elite of achievers got to experience each and every day. He mulled over whether it was about social class, contacts, wealth or something else entirely: who and what you actually are.

There were a couple of youngish men and one girl on his client list who all had their details entered in blue. Julian had no doubt they would all have their funds cleared and settled in the next few days as they had seemed very well to do. He had a group nickname for them: 'the trustfunders'. In truth they all worked or did something resembling work (one even had a job in banking) but he got the strong sense that family money was somehow a significant part of their lifestyle. He had met them all at the same place: a stylish new members' club that had opened up just over a year ago in West London. The lighting was dim and tinged with purple. It had run a discreet advertisement in a couple of the glossy monthlies Stephanie read: "If you have made it or are making it in the arts, media or finance, or are just good company and a fan of well put together cocktails, register here to meet others on your wavelength." It is bad form for a club to tout for new members, but Julian had liked the direct, cheeky approach and signed up. He realised it would soon be time for another visit.

Anyway, it was time to go. Time for a nice family lunch – the sort you cannot wait to end. He got up and walked over to the door. As he pulled it the complete lack of resistance told him someone on the other side was pushing it. It was a girl, somewhere in her early twenties, slim and, at a tad over five foot, on the small side. Her dark brunette bob and milk chocolate coloured eyes suggested she was related to the owner – a niece perhaps? Plain black jeans and a halter top gave her the impression of a waitress; maybe a student doing holiday shifts for some extra cash. But the bulky paperback in her hand told the casual observer that she was about to indulge in a lengthy, coffee fuelled reading session. She glanced expressionlessly at Julian as they walked past each other. As she edged past the other patrons in the crowded café, many just getting up to leave, he was struck by how deftly her slim wrist and fingers manoeuvred the oversized novel. She found the emptiest possible stretch of seating, plonked the book on the table top and looked as if she wouldn't look upwards for the next several hours. Julian said "excuse me" as he walked past a tall man in a long coat who was standing at the entrance and tried to guess what title her book was, running through some of the lengthier classics in his head. He didn't think mass market fiction would be her style at all.

He found himself walking somewhat more briskly on the way home, and not just because the journey was downhill. He had just filled his head with almost every human and economic reality his business encompassed and he was aware now of an odd sensation: that somehow, in the open air, between the familiar bases of Café Franz and home, some of it might be seeping out into the atmosphere. There were normal, good people walking around. Other sorts, too. Some of them would be able to pick up on a little disturbance here and there, the odd whiff. He quickened his pace.

As he neared his house he saw through the kitchen window that Stephanie was darting about animatedly from stove to worktop, more making sure that everything was in order than actually preparing food. She paid particular, motherly attention to two saucepans, one large, the other somewhat diminutive, both simmering satisfactorily. Much further back, near the door that adjoined the dining room, stood her parents, watching her with calm smiles and shining eyes. Julian opened the front door and walked inside. Clive and Kathleen Huntley stepped out of the kitchen and met him in the corridor.

"Clive! Kath! Hey, good to see you both. How was your journey? Awful traffic around here, I'll bet? Anyway, glad you finally made it."

Clive held out a large, fleshy hand and Julian took that as permission to shake it. "Hello Julian. How's business these days? Still making money with your... financial *wizardry*?" Clive was tall and heavily built with thick, centre parted and back combed white hair. Any original handsomeness had long ago been overpowered by a decade or two of eating rather too well, and presently by a shirt, tie and pocket kerchief all in the same shade of salmon. His shapely and elegant wife, roughly ten years younger, had apparently been gifted to him by the gods of style and good taste, eager to make amends.

Looking at him, Julian couldn't understand why he held Clive in such high regard. He eventually said, "Yes. Pretty good. I'm really quite pleased with the strategy. The way it's all going at the moment."

"Glad to hear it. Stephanie does seem happy right now, and that's the main thing I'm interested in, as you well know. Perhaps you might get round to proposing to her. Why not, eh?" Kath's eyes rolled.

"Absolutely. Perhaps – when you have the time, you might get round to sending me your starting cheque? I've still got you down as pending." Julian's request got lost in a busy, clattering sound. All three turned to look.

Stephanie came out of the kitchen carrying a serving dish. She walked briskly, taking tiny steps, as if to emphasise its heat and weight. "Do please sit down, all of you. Lunch is served, as of now! I hope you're all in the mood to be adventurous gourmets. I know Julian always is." Her usually bare feet were now contained in a pair of well used fawn ballet flats, her favourites.

Kath said, "Luckily for you, your father will eat anything, preferably in large amounts".

13

"So Clive, what about you? How's the barbeque business?" said Julian.

Only the corners of Clive's mouth moved, venturing upwards. He was on his second glass of wine. The others had barely had a sip. "As I always say, if you can make a living persuading people to cook and eat outdoors in a country that rains ten months of the year, well, you could probably sell" – he looked at his glass – "English wine to the French." They all laughed except Clive, who looked intently at Julian. "You might say I'm *quite pleased with the strategy*. It's taken me a long time to build up this business. About twenty-eight years." He leaned back in his chair and glanced at each diner in turn, looking a little too long and hard at Julian. "I remember how it all started. I was cold calling, knocking on doors. But I had to do it. Had to become independent."

Julian nodded, a little too vigorously. "There's nothing like the power of being independent, the – the freedom, you know, of being your own man. No boss to answer to".

"Indeed. But Julian, you started off as an engineer. Don't you miss it? That creativity, combined with exactness?" Clive smiled. "Although you do still have that old car. That must require some mechanical intervention."

A neighbour's car alarm went off suddenly and noisily. It pulsated and whined, finally dying away after thirty seconds.

"That's right," Stephanie eventually said. "When I met Julian he was working as an engineer and just seemed like a really down to earth sort of guy. He was still using

14

his old name back then, Jonathan Kiel. I suppose Julian Kay's not bad – it does sound more like a financial advisor, more upmarket." She had a resigned look on her face.

"Kiel, now that name's got character. Where was it you two met?" asked Kath. "A bookshop, right? I mean, you studied Romance languages with history, didn't you darling? Interesting how opposites do attract, so often in life."

"We met at a book *club* actually, but yes, it was being held at a bookshop. Hamble's in fact, just up here on the high street". Stephanie pointed in a random direction, but roughly upwards.

"A techie who's also literate. Now, that's what I call a catch," said Kath.

"But have you seen him in the kitchen? Stay out, for your own sake!" said Stephanie, interrupting the laughter.

Before meeting him, Stephanie had worked for a translation agency specialising in transaction documentation for companies doing business across Latin America. She had achieved a senior position (in what was, admittedly, a very small company) but left rather suddenly to start a restaurant. It had specialised in Mexican cuisine – *real* Mexican food, she had insisted – and survived for a couple of years before she lost interest. When Julian had met her she had been living with her parents and wondering what to do next. He imagined her enjoying her parents' attention, money and fuss; waking up late and doing what she wanted, which often meant nothing.

Julian thought of his own parents and how he had been brought up as an only child. His father had been an overbearing man, dependable financially but unable to see his softly spoken mother's point of view. He had refused to pay for or go on family holidays, leaving her to save up her part time secretary's salary to take Julian to the seaside, and later to nearby capitals on the continent. She was determined that he would go to university and supported him financially while he was there reading mechanical engineering, ignoring his father's view that higher education was a waste of time and gave children unrealistic expectations. Julian's overwhelming memory of his teenage years was of reading anything he could get his hands on: library books or second hand paperbacks; fantasies, romances, books on mathematics, physics and the lives of great inventors; Russian and French classics in translation, Dickens, Conrad, Borges and Nabokov. His own novel remained hardly one third written, rendered on scraps of lined writing pad paper and assorted computer text files, the latter very confusingly named. His father had often helpfully suggested that he should devote more time to finding a girlfriend than "scribbling". But there was one subject on which his parents had been in total agreement: that he must get a job, a steady, reliable and preferably well paid one and not get too carried away with his hobbies.

Just before Stephanie's parents were about to leave, Julian thanked Clive for referring Paul Kelmer. "Thanks for putting a good word in for me. He signed up this morning."

Clive looked puzzled. "You mean your investment scheme? Never mentioned it to Paul Kelmer. No, he does my books for the business, but that's done through the limited company. My investment with you is strictly on the personal account. He said I recommended you?"

Julian drifted off for a second, trying to remember exactly what Paul had said. Clive looked at him warily and jangled his car keys. "You're more famous than you realise."

As their Mercedes hummed into the distance, Julian helped Steph clear the table and fill the dishwasher. She thought her curry had gone down pretty well, and to be truthful Julian had helped himself to the largest serving. Eating more had become a consequence of drinking less, as if his physical being were seeking compensation with something almost as sinful. As she listed various alternative spice combinations for future experimentation, now and then asking him what he thought, Julian remembered a friend with whom he had spent quite a lot of time at university and for a couple of years afterwards. Feeling the need for some fresh air, he stepped outside and texted him.

He got a reply roughly five minutes later. "Hey Jules. Long time, no speak. You still living in this neck of the woods? What do you say to real ale, real talk, one hour from now – plan?"

Julian didn't believe a better plan existed. He texted back: "You're on, Rob. Railway @ four?"

Rob Jollison replied: "Yep. That's the pub at the bottom of the high street, right? See you there." Julian had met up with him last year, when Rob had been renting a room in a shared house. Julian wondered how he was managing with the relentless rise in rents across London and this neighbourhood in particular.

"Jules!" Rob called out from the bar as soon as Julian had walked in through the heavy stained wood and glass pub doors. He had a cheerful grin on his small, round face, but as Julian walked towards him he exchanged it for a humorously mocking pout. "You've been ignoring me. I see your old friends don't quite cut the mustard any more. And *just* when I'd started getting used to calling you Julian!"

Julian smiled half-heartedly; he had wanted to appear more elated at meeting Rob but felt guilty about the scant attention he'd being paying him these last few months. He had told him nothing about the investment scheme he'd been running, and besides, Rob was far too straightforward to suspect him, or anyone else, of any scheming. As someone who was barely managing to pay his rent and bills, Julian knew that Rob's status of true friend would never be spoiled by any possibility of him becoming a client. Julian decided to relax and enjoy their real passion together: English ales. Rob was small but his almost spherical figure always reassured him he was something of a beer expert, and an ideal companion with whom he could enjoy his self-imposed allowance of two pints per week. There had been a time when Julian would limit his drinking in order to save money. These days it was far more about control.

"I really am happy for you," Rob was saying. "That career change. Switching jobs like that. Real stroke of genius." Julian always sensed that Rob considered financial success to be something determined by the heavens: if it came to you, well and good; if not, so what? Money wasn't something to lose sleep (or drinking time) over.

Rob appeared to be mulling something over. "Jonathan Kiel. Julian Kay. Yes, I see. I like what you did with that name change. It just sounds like money, you know, Surrey stockbroker belt and all that. Myself, I'm still stuck in engineering, but I suppose I deserve it."

"Still designing lift motors?" Julian always wondered why Rob had stuck to the same small firm that grossly underpaid him.

"Yep, that's me. I still get a buzz out of it, would you believe. After all these years."

"Where do you live now, Rob? I know you're still in this area but is it that same studio room?"

"Ah, well, funny you should ask. I'm just about to move. It's the same sized room but the shared house I'll be in is a lot bigger. A sort of palace, really. Only uglier than an actual palace. You know that hill you go up – the one *you* go up – when you're walking from where you live to up here? Well, it's just off that hill. A street full of enormous houses. Hobart Road, yes, that's it. A few of them still have rooms for letting out and I managed to get one. Would've been the servants' quarters back in the old days." He had started looking around the main seating area of the pub, where groups of girls from their late teens to mid-twenties were sharing bottles of wine. Rosé seemed to predominate. "Looks like The Railway's revamped itself, eh? A few years ago it would've only been old men like us".

Julian had come here to relax. "Rob, do you remember that time at university when we got those home brewing kits? We got hold of about ten of them and it didn't quite, er, turn out as we expected?"

A look of delight lit up Rob's face and he looked as if he were stifling a guffaw. "Oh my god. Yes, how could I forget? Something definitely went wrong there. It didn't help that the instructions were in Czech. I don't think I've ever had so much gas in my life!"

"Seriously embarrassing. And to cap it all we went to that party afterwards. Right after that huge session. It was probably the best party all year – all those cute fresher girls, do you remember? And the state we were in. I left early."

"Yes, me too. That was one wasted opportunity!" agreed Rob, taking a particularly large gulp of pale ale. "Anyway, you've sorted yourself out, that's for sure. You hardly touch a drop these days! Once again, Jules, I've got to hand it to you. You're really laughing now."

Despite the laughter, Julian had a tight feeling in his chest, paired with a loose one in his stomach. A fragment of his old life had just been injected intravenously, like a sedative, into this demanding new one. He knew that in the weeks and months from now he might well be looking back at this jolly meeting, possibly from a far darker place, as the happiest of times. He finished his ale, put a hand on Rob's shoulder, and then walked towards the door, hoping that Rob would still be living nearby the next time he needed his company.

The light outside told him it was early evening. Twilight was Julian's favourite time of the day, when the sun's light seemed to relax, not illuminating but merely playing with people, buildings and trees. Before heading back he decided to watch the office workers making their way home from the tube station. They looked dishevelled, with half undone ties, hanging out shirts and cheap shoes. There were some schoolchildren too, teenagers who had no particular curfew to abide by or, apparently, homework to do, so lounged in cafes in their school uniforms until dark.

Then he saw *her* again: the small girl who liked big books. He caught sight of her slender frame and perfect, helmet like dark bob as she came past, seeing her face only in profile. He imagined it as motionless as it was in Café Franz that morning. With her was a much older man, tall, well built with an almost shaven head. He was wearing a long leather coat, which seemed to emphasise his rapid, furious strides. As she struggled to keep up, Julian noticed he was holding her hand very tightly, but no fingers were intertwined; rather, he seemed to be gripping her wrist, dragging her forward. Some girls have curious taste in men, Julian reflected, shaking his head as he walked home.

Chapter 2

A couple of evenings later, Julian found himself sitting at the long, curved bar of the Westway House members club. The bar was made of stained wood with a pink marble top. Its surface consisted of different sections, some plain marble, others made up of interlocking strips of wood and marble producing a striking visual effect. Next to him, half seated on a bar stool with one foot placed securely on the floor, slouched one of Julian's more recent clients: a very overweight young man by the name of Miles Frederick. Miles was dressed in a tan suit with bold magenta checks, which helped somewhat to focus attention away from his fat laden cheeks and sparse reddish hair. The top button of his tieless white shirt was undone, revealing sporadic strands of chest hair, lighter in colour than the ones growing from his scalp. Mercifully it was only the top button that was unfastened tonight. Julian considered exposure to such curious fauna alone to be worth Westway House's annual membership fee.

"The thing about work experience," Miles was explaining, "is that it's only really a genuine experience if it actually *feels* like work. But it never does with me. So listen: dad interrupts me one day when I was just about to take the Lamborghini out for a good hammering. Damned inconvenient timing. Anyway, he seems to think that toiling in his chain of health spas – me, health spas? Ha! – would be a good way for me to make something of my life. He didn't say exactly what he wanted me to make it into, but clearly he thought being surrounded by lots of skinny yoga chicks and over muscled men would have a beneficial effect." He looked from left to right, then back at Julian, and said in a quieter voice "Must admit though, some damn attractive young ladies there!" and started giggling softly. Miles was a local resident. Financed by his property developer father, he lived in a small, architecturally impeccable cream stucco fronted period building roughly a quarter of a mile from Westway House. He was a regular at the club and took his quota of exercise by walking there virtually every other evening at around nine o'clock. Julian imagined the gentle, rolling bounce of his hips that must have accompanied his unhurried gait.

The barman deftly placed their drinks on two small white napkins: a gin and tonic for Julian and a strawberry frozen margarita for Miles, who had told Julian that cocktails with added fruit were nutritious and contributed to one's dietary fibre requirement. A friendly nod from Julian served as thanks to the barman and an instruction to add the cost to his bar tab. Miles continued, "You see I've got private means, and that's why simply being at work never really feels like proper work. I just don't need to be there for the money, unlike the others, the regular folk who have all those real bills to pay. And kids too, I'll bet. I suppose dad thinks I need to spend time with his employees to learn about real life. I say you haven't lived real life until you've floored a turbo down a country road. I mean, they're all nice enough people to work with but really I've got better things to do. Fast cars don't drive themselves you know."

"No, I don't suppose they do." Julian considered it odd how whenever he met people with practically unlimited amounts of free time they never did anything with it that he would. He had spent most of his early life and career being unaware that people like Miles really existed. He had heard about such types of course but didn't think he'd ever get to know one. As soon as he had met Stephanie characters like Miles Frederick, although perhaps not quite as visually striking, had started making an appearance at the fringes of their social life. Stephanie had many friends who did nothing, often very luxuriously, although always insisted that she herself needed to keep busy "doing something worthwhile". On and off, that was partly true. He believed that without the influence of some of her best friends she would have more success at sticking to projects. If she ever met Miles she would hit it off with him at once, probably taking him under her wing like a wayward younger brother. Of course, Julian hadn't the slightest intention

25

of telling Stephanie about any of his new friends at Westway House.

Miles was sitting straighter now, with both feet on the bar stool's crossbar. "You know what Julian? I'm so glad you and I met. People like you with great investment ideas are what I really need in my life right now. It's all about *diversification*. My trust fund allowance, sure, that's okay for now but I have to think of the future. I need something that's really mine. Independently within my control, if you follow me?" Julian nodded slowly. Miles continued, "After all, my dad could change his mind and cut me off any day. You never know." He fell silent for a few seconds, and looked at Julian sombrely. But before the mood had a chance to become too depressing, members of the jazz trio that the club had hired for the evening got to their feet and, without a word of introduction, launched into a rather rapid rendition of Herbie Hancock's *Cantaloupe*. It seemed to take everyone in the club by surprise. Miles perked up, lumbered to his feet and began to move in time to the music. His head moved back and forth, his shoulders rotated like the piston driven wheels of a steam locomotive as he mechanically shifted his weight from one foot to the other and back again. His huge body moved very little, which Julian considered a particularly energy efficient – and as far as innocent bystanders were concerned, safe – way of dancing. As Miles' attention was drawn away by a group of tight jeaned, long haired young women who had begun dancing with one another, Julian started thinking about somebody he had been reading about, a notorious businessman-turned-swindler from a century ago, who both scared and fascinated him.

In 1903 a young man called Charles Ponzi arrived in Boston, Massachusetts from a small town in Italy with "two bucks fifty-four in my pocket and a million dollars in my heart." That certainly sounds like the beginning of a heart-warming immigrant success story, Julian thought. And for a while, Charles Ponzi was probably the most celebrated success that early twentieth century America had to feast on. After a succession of frustrating jobs washing dishes and waiting tables in restaurants, Ponzi managed to get a job as a bank teller at an Italian owned bank catering mainly to recent immigrants who were not comfortable speaking English. The bank just happened to pay savers double the interest rate that any other bank offered. The long, happy queues of depositors set Ponzi's mind working: he knew that each eager new customer's funds would be used to pay 'interest' to earlier ones. How could he do this for himself, pocketing a generous cut in the process? Of course the missing link was the idea to sell to the public: he needed to persuade them that the profits were coming from a legitimate investment. The gap was soon filled when he stumbled upon the international postal reply coupon. This humble postage paid slip enabled a sender of goods in one country to pre pay the return postage of the receiver based in another country if he wished to return the goods. And here was the trick: the return postage was paid at the local rate in the sender's country but redeemed at the rate prevailing in the receiver's country. So somebody just needed to find two countries in which the mailing fee differed by a large amount and he could make a lot of free money by buying in the cheaper country and redeeming in the dearer. Pretty clever, thought Julian.

Ponzi wasted no time. He hired a smart suite of offices in Boston's Lexington Avenue and placed a simply worded advertisement in the city's newspaper: "Our expertise in trading international reply coupons could significantly increase your capital. Achieve guaranteed returns of 50% in 90 days." The initial trickle of investors soon turned into a frenzy once excited clients realised just how easy it was to get rich. Ponzi himself upgraded his residence to a mansion in the city's best street and relished his new role as a popular public figure. He was raising the present day equivalent of millions of dollars every month, and believed he deserved the lifestyle to match such impressive numbers. Of course, he had long forgotten about the postal coupons themselves; the flood of new investors provided all the cash flow he needed. A number of journalists, and later a financial regulator, began to ask questions: the profits implied that over a hundred million reply coupons had been redeemed, although according to the postal authorities in the countries concerned, only a few tens of thousands had ever been issued. But the public was simply not interested. They wanted to get rich and regarded the probing authority figures as annoying busybodies.

Julian admired Ponzi's pluck but regarded him as naïve, greedy and irresponsible. There was a world of difference between himself – educated, cultured, modest and above all, discreet – and a brash, vulgar immigrant who grew too big, too fast and spent money to compensate for a lack of class. Ponzi did have one distinction that Julian realised he'd never achieve. Even though he ended up living a life of poverty following deportation to Italy (he had never acquired US citizenship) Ponzi gave his name to eternity: every rob-peter-to-pay-paul pyramid scheme is known today as a Ponzi scheme. That's one he's welcome to, Julian thought, smiling. No, what set Julian apart from the *average swindler* (Julian hated both those words when there was the merest suggestion of them being used to describe him) was self-control. Some upmarket charm too, without a doubt, as well as the ability to keep things on a manageable scale, not to draw unnecessary attention to oneself and, whilst offering impressive profits, not promising anything too outlandish. Julian reclined a little on the low backed barstool and started nodding slowly and gently to himself, fully digesting the facts. Yes, he was probably going to be in business for a long time.

He then became aware of a slim hand that had been placed lightly on his shoulder, almost touching his neck. He jolted forward, not quite spilling his gin and tonic but doing a thorough job of splashing his nose and inhaling some of it. He turned his head to see who it was. A good looking face framed by mousey hair, belonging to a woman approximately thirty-five years old, smiled back at him. "Hello Julian. Sorry, didn't mean to scare you like that. You were miles away!" she said. "Deep in thought. Planning your next hugely profitable strike on the global financial markets, no doubt." Her eyes darted around the bar for some paper napkins and, locating them, she handed him one.

"Hi, Heather, good to see you. You're looking well." Her normally light olive skin looked bronzed and slightly pink, in a rather attractive way. Overall she appeared fresher than when he had last seen her. The frown lines seemed to have been ironed out by the holiday that she had evidently just been on.

"Yes, my tan's fading now. Thought I'd show if off here a bit before it completely disappears on me."

"Did you go anywhere glamorous?" Julian asked. Heather was a former model who in her twenties had done extremely well posing for glossy magazine advertisements and store catalogues. By her early thirties work had all but dried up, but her taste for exotic holidays and fine living, including a drug habit that several stays in expensive therapy centres hadn't had any effect on, remained robust. When she wasn't in a nightclub her evenings seemed to consist of accompanying much older men to formal restaurants and elegant cocktail bars. It hadn't surprised Julian that she'd been one of the first members of Westway House (second only to Miles, who had been advertising Julian's genius to the club's regulars) to sign up for his investment scheme. Which reminded him: right now would be the perfect time to ask her about the cheque for her initial deposit. Obviously the holiday had got in the way of that.

"We've been back a week now," she continued. "Barbados. We rented a small house for a fortnight. It was heavenly, just what we both needed."

"Ah yes, you and Oliver. The Harley Street guy. Private cardiologist, right?"

She smiled guiltily and looked away. "Er, no, actually. I'm not with him anymore. I went to the Caribbean with my new boyfriend, Toby – I don't think you've met him. This is his first time here. I'm not sure what he thinks."

"He's here tonight?"

"Yes, he just stepped outside for a smoke." Julian suddenly felt the need to get up and walk around outside. The air in the club was getting stale. "He's a policeman, you know." Julian raised his eyebrows. "Yes, that's right. Well, a detective, actually." She smiled wanly to acknowledge her newly acquired status in the dating market: from sybaritic millionaires to upstanding but financially struggling government employees. "We're semi-serious already. I really appreciate him taking me on holiday."

He must have been saving up, Julian thought. "So anyway Heather, how's work? I've heard the wedding business is booming these days?" Heather had tried, surprisingly hard in fact, to find steady employment after the demise of her modelling career. After several jobs in small modern art galleries and a genuine attempt to become a 'negotiator' at an upmarket estate agency, she had eventually found something she was doing fairly well at: selling, or rather advising on, hugely overpriced wedding gowns from a tiny shop in one of London's priciest post codes.

"Well, the sales are coming in, that's for sure. I can't complain, but what really makes me wonder is the sort of girls you see marrying rich men nowadays. Usually nerdy IT entrepreneurs, the odd hedge fund manager, guys like that. They seem to be choosing women who are... well, who have no looks at all, sort of overweight, not pretty. Some even have acne. Maybe they really are in love, who knows?"

Julian nodded. "Yes. Funny, isn't it? Love being blind and all that. Listen, Heather – about your investment. I've still got you down as pending from more than a month ago. You are definitely going ahead, aren't you? It's just that I'd need the cheque, or better still a bank transfer, pretty soon if that's okay?"

Heather's face fell, and for the first time that evening her old frown lines made an appearance. "Actually Julian, I've decided not to go ahead."

"Oh really?" Julian was both surprised and disappointed, but showed neither emotion on his face.

She looked down for a second, then said "I've been talking it over with Toby. I was very keen, as you well know, but Toby raised two important points. Firstly, since we're probably going to find a place together quite soon, now probably isn't the best time to be making major investments– "

"Sure. Understood. It's just a shame you can't benefit from these exceptional returns we've had. Moving home can be a pricey business."

"Yes, that is true. Secondly, Toby tends to be extremely careful about any kind of investment. Not surprisingly he's never actually made any. Typical over cautious cop! Plus, I suppose he's never really had that much spare cash. Anyway he likes to do a lot of research before parting with money and he'd want to sit down with you and pick your brains for hours. If you fancy your chances you could give it a shot."

An interview with a detective? Hmm, no thanks, Julian thought. "You're probably right, Heather. Best to leave a decision like this until you've settled in and know how much you've got to spare. Any questions, don't hesitate to call me." He felt he was taking this far harder than any of the other rejections he had got. Heather had been considering a fairly small investment which would have made virtually no difference to his scheme, but she herself was different. For a start she would have been his only female client. He had also really wanted to help her, partly because he found her attractive, but also because she seemed to be down on her luck. Julian remembered the days he had been there all too clearly. He wondered how much of the decision had been due to Toby's influence and how much was Heather's natural feminine sense of caution.

Just then the band members stood up, announced it was time for some "sweet romance" and began to play a slow, syrupy number with wide eyed expressions of tenderness on their faces, exaggerated for comic effect. Miles, who had been lurking a few feet away, grabbed Heather by the shoulders from behind and began gyrating. Laughing, she joined in, ensuring a vital few inches of space between them was maintained at all times. Julian knew this was his chance to step outside for some air. He raised his hand and nodded to Heather and Miles, then walked towards the exit and descended the stairs.

"Hell*oo*, boss!" said a hearty, friendly voice at the street exit. It was Harry, the West Indian doorman. "Lots of pretty ladies in tonight, for sure."

"Hey Harry. Yes indeed. It was absolutely heaving up there."

"Perfect for a well-dressed rascal like you. Hope you had fun, my friend."

Julian grinned at Harry and walked away to the side of the building, the unadorned, windowless end of terrace wall where smokers seeking solitude or a discreet conversation went to escape the voluble crowds at the club's entrance. Julian had never smoked a cigarette (that is, a normal tobacco one) in his life, but this wall was one of his favourite places. He looked around at the sparse groupings of smokers and lingerers: young women with sleek hair, dandyishly dressed men with trimmed beards, a sprinkling of hipsters in tight black sweaters.

Then he saw him, leaning against the wall, right at the end. Dark, tousled hair with significant amounts of grey. A youngish, square face staring, frozen, into the distance. A half smoked cigarette in his hand, which seemed to have extinguished itself hours ago, gave him the appearance of an intellectual deep in thought. Or, someone trying to sober up after one drink too many.

"Hi. Toby, isn't it? I'm Julian, a friend of Heather's."

He turned round, paused, then smiled. "Yes, that's right. Toby Marks. Pleased to meet you." Julian shook his hand. "It's actually detective chief inspector Marks from nine to five; Heather may have told you?"

"She did, yes. Good to meet you, Toby."

"And you're the investment expert, right? I've heard some impressive things."

"Ya, well, I look after people's money, some other stuff too. So, er, how's the force these days? I'm sure it's been pretty tough lately, with all those cuts looming?"

"Can't say I've noticed much difference really. Detectives work long hours anyway. When a case is going on it's just expected of you, especially if it's high profile and the pressure is on. I doubt they'll reduce our overtime, but, well, nine to five is really a joke in our job." He looked more interestedly at Julian. "Same in your line of work, right? Financial markets, all that stress. I can imagine the work never stops."

Julian nodded hard. "It can be very stressful at times. So – this place – Westway House. What do you think of it? I must say you're the first copper I've met here."

"It's fun actually. I thought it would be pretentious and I'd hate it, but I've actually come to quite like it. Heather's been a regular for ages so I thought I'd put the effort in and show up now and then; that's how it grew on me. Actually coming here tonight was my idea. One thing though: the drinks prices. They're a complete rip off."

"Yes, they're exorbitant." Julian smiled slyly. "You know, you might find your workload increasing if you spend any more time here. There are some pretty suspect characters on the membership. Well worth investigating, some of them."

Toby chuckled, then looked at his watch. "Actually, I was about to head off. Heather's going to make a night of it here but I've got a fairly early start tomorrow morning." He looked as if he had thought of something, then raised his index finger. "You live in north London, don't you?"

"That's right."

"Heather told me. I'm heading that way myself, just a bit further out than you. If you fancy a lift, I could drop you off somewhere convenient?"

"Thanks, that would be great" said Julian. "Where's your car?" A three minute walk to the end of the street revealed two headlights staring at him like the compound eyes on a fly's head. It was a small, pristine sports car from a couple of decades ago. "Wow. That's gorgeous. A 1970s Porsche?"

"Huh, yes, my pride and joy. It's the 911S. It basically explains how a man can get to my age and not own a house. Oh well, this is more fun, some would say."

"Is it Cream? Or Light yellow?"

"Orange" corrected Toby. "But we're standing under an orange street lamp right now. That's why it looks white."

"Of course." Julian climbed carefully into the cramped passenger seat and braced himself for twenty minutes or so of noisy engine surges and queasily sharp turns. Neither said anything for several minutes. Eventually Julian asked "Where did you two meet?"

"Wine tasting event."

"Uh-huh. Nice." There followed an extended period of automotive lurching, growling and screeching. Julian held lightly onto the base of his seat. He gradually became aware that Toby was saying something, or rather muttering to himself, but in fact Julian could clearly distinguish every word.

"Three percent per month. Hmm. Five percent maybe. How does he do it? How can it be done? Clever. Ever so clever..."

Julian froze. "Pardon?" he said. Either he or Toby had had a little too much to drink.

"Oh, nothing Julian, sorry. I was just thinking out loud. Heather and I are trying to find a place together right now. I was just going over rental versus mortgage options, you know, interest rates, best deals, that sort of thing."

"Right. Of course." He waited for three more surges of anger from the engine, counting them on his fingers as they gripped the seat, then took a deep breath and asked "And what about investments? Considering any homes for your money?" Success, thought Julian, often involves venturing as close to danger as you can, proving you are not scared. Good things had usually happened to him when he'd pushed himself beyond the point he thought would trigger an asthma attack. A cop on his client list would be the perfect stamp of respectability.

Toby's eyebrows lifted up. "Well. Investments, I should be so lucky. You might say it's a bit of a cash flow problem right now. What with this antique and all our moving expenses."

"Yes, I know what you mean. Seems like it's been ages since Stephanie and I went through that."

"But don't worry, I will eventually get round to looking at your proposal. It's just a case of finding the time. But, mark my words, I'll get onto it. I will investigate it thoroughly."

Julian wondered just how deep his investigation would go. As an underpaid state employee with an expensive new lifestyle to finance, Toby was far more likely to be lured in by the big profits. He leaned back in the passenger seat and enjoyed the ride, observing the gradual shift in street lighting and shop frontage from central London to the inner suburbs. After what seemed like an hour Toby said "Okay, looks like we've made some great progress up the Finchley Road. The traffic would have been a nightmare during daytime, don't you reckon? So, where can I drop you off?"

Julian wanted to make sure Toby didn't find out which street he lived on – not tonight, anyway. On the other hand, he didn't want to be stranded miles away, leaving him with a half hour walk home. Instinctively he thought of Rob's new street. "Third right from here. You should be able to turn right at the next lights."

"Ah yes, I do know the street. Ho–"

"Yes, that's the one," said Julian, "awfully big houses, not always in the best taste. Not that I live there, ha! My place is a couple of roads away, but it's a pain to get to with all the parked cars."

Toby pulled up and stopped the engine. There was an uneasy but refreshing silence, as if the two men had driven deep into the countryside north of London. Julian listened as the earliest morning birds began to chirp, and looked around for a scavenging fox. None appeared. Toby began surveying the nearby streets with an air of familiarity and knowledge. "I've been doing quite a bit of work around here recently. There's a lot that's been keeping me busy in this neck of the woods, would you believe."

"Is that right?" Julian wondered what felonies concealed themselves inside the mansions which themselves hid behind the giant, ancient trees that lined the streets. Crimes of passion, maybe? Who knew what well-groomed lady of leisure was capable of doing after enough botox and liposuction. He leaned forward in the bucket seat.

"Actually, yes. Do you know much about London's major criminal families?" Julian simply looked blank. "I'll take that as a no. There's no particular reason why you should, is there? Anyway, most of London's big crime syndicates are headed by respected members of the community. Or so you would think. They seem pretty damn respectable on the surface. We're talking about middle aged men – and women, too – who are sitting on schools' governors' boards, the local Rotarians, you name it. They're holding smart dinner parties in their beautiful homes, giving money to art foundations, religious charities and scholarship funds."

"I see," said Julian. "So, what's going on?"

Toby sniffed. "Gangsters, all of them. Sure, they've got legitimate businesses going on: real estate, property rentals, garages, restaurants, you name it. And they're clever enough to make everything else they're doing look legit, by putting it all through the books as something else. Things like drugs, extortion, loan sharking. All cash businesses, you might say. Ha. Some nasty people. They've killed, got blood on their hands, no doubt about that. But whom? Damned if we've got a shred of evidence." Julian undid his seatbelt and opened the door. "And on that note," sighed Toby, "it's probably time to say goodnight." He held out his hand and Julian clasped it.

"Thanks, Toby. Thanks so much for the lift. I hope you and Heather find a really nice place at a great price. Really, I wish you the best of luck." Julian meant that sincerely. He hoped Heather found somewhere that would make her happy; she really deserved a break. But he wasn't entirely sure what to make of Toby. He was an ordinary, hard-working policeman with a pleasant manner, probably quite clever too. But his intellect had taken a different route from Julian's. It was focussed on detecting and weeding out the immoral and the criminal, whereas Julian preferred a freer, more utilitarian relationship with those purely social constructs. Could he be trusted, Julian wondered. Would he ever become a friend?

As he walked home, Julian thought about what it would be like to be the head of a major criminal organisation. All that power and respect. But, no doubt, the role came with great risk. If you spent your life destroying people, what might eventually happen to you? Realising that his own achievements, by comparison, were still fairly insignificant and that actually to date he had only been making people happier, he strode home briskly and cheerfully, inhaling deep lungfuls of the cooling night air.

Chapter 3

The next morning Julian woke up early, made his own cup of tea and immediately went into his study (the smallest of the four bedrooms, perfectly square and windowless) to focus on the older, conventional, or, as conventionally minded people would say, legitimate part of his business: pensions advice. Those two words seemed amusingly archaic to him these days. The activity itself was an annoying irrelevance, but he had some documentation to finish and was determined to complete it in less than an hour. He needed to concentrate; Julian always found that boring tasks dragged on forever, mysteriously expanding in scope and complexity.

Some busy, playful, happy noises were coming from the kitchen. Julian looked up from his regulatory paperwork and listened. Suddenly there was a loud, clanging clatter of saucepans falling on the floor, and two female voices burst out laughing. Needing a break from his form filling, Julian got up and went downstairs to find out what was going on. He stood in the arch at the kitchen's entrance and leaned against the frame. There was an unfamiliar but pleasant smell permeating the small space: aromatic and mildly spicy, with an undertone of expensive floral perfume. Julian prided himself on having committed a large number of feminine scents to memory (Stephanie had an impressive collection) but this was one he hadn't inhaled before. There was no evidence of the great cooking utensil collapse from a few minutes ago apart from a small, dark brown puddle on the floor, which looked as if it had been far larger prior to an unfinished act of mopping up. The two women ignored what was left just enough to avoid putting a foot in it.

Stephanie and her friend Allegra appeared to be hard at work. What they were doing was clearly highly experimental and original. There was a scattered pile of Indian cookery books, some of which were lying open, at one end of the long worktop and at the other were eight or ten sheets of lined A4 notepaper, torn roughly from an abandoned writing pad. The paper had been energetically scrawled on, in handwriting that Julian couldn't recognise. It was round and florid, with huge loops on the tails of the g's and y's.

Julian had walked down to the kitchen softy. Neither his silk dressing gown nor slippers had made a sound. As soon as the two women noticed that a curious

44

man in his dressing gown was observing them, both turned to look at him. Stephanie pursed her lips and raised her eyebrows, which said "I thought you were hard at work?" Then she said out loud, "Hey, you. You have met my friend Allegra, haven't you?"

Allegra didn't wait for him to answer. She sauntered over, carefully making sure the wiggle of her hips wasn't too obvious. She lifted her arms slowly and placed her wrists on his shoulders, palms facing down. Her scarlet, long nailed fingers still had some remnants of food preparation on them, and Allegra skilfully kept them away from his silk dressing gown. She looked intently into his eyes. Her small nose and wide set blue eyes reminded Julian of a child. "Of course, Julian and I have met. Haven't we, darling? I really don't think I'd forget any man this handsome." Stephanie made some sort of facial expression that eventually turned into a tight smile. Julian felt glad he'd done a thorough job of brushing his teeth.

"Allegra, hello. Yes, of course, we have met. Once, I think. You were at university with Steph?"

"Yes, she was a mature student at the time," said Stephanie helpfully.

Allegra removed her arms from Julian's shoulders. "That's right, I was a couple of years ahead of Stephie. I started there when I was twenty-one. Luckily we are still twenty-one, in a manner of speaking. At least, in here." She tapped her temple with a knuckle.

"So, what are you both up to? Looks like you're concocting some new kind of curry."

"New kind of cuisine, to be exact," said Stephanie. "Paleo-Indian. That is, a low carb version of Indian food. Imagine being able to eat all the curry you want and not put on weight. At least, that's the theory. We need to work on it more. I think it's going to be all the rage."

"That's right," continued Allegra. "Paleo means as stone age man would have eaten. Pre-agriculture, you basically had to eat whatever you could kill or gather from the forest. That's the way we should all be eating today."

"And to help the world with that," said Stephanie "Allegra and I are working on creating the first low carb restaurant dedicated to Indian food."

"That's a great idea," said Julian, immediately realising the consequences of his enthusiasm.

"Glad you think so. Because you do know who our major investor is going to be, don't you?" They both giggled and pointed at him. "Money as well as looks," said Allegra softly.

"Right, yes," Julian answered drearily. "I'll be backing you all the way."

"There's something we haven't told you," continued Stephanie. "We're going away for a week on a residential restaurant management course. It's going to be about menu development, financial management, hiring and retaining staff, that sort of thing. Loads of vital stuff for surviving your first year in the business." Julian looked at them both suspiciously. "Come on Julian," said Stephanie, "It's not going to cost you that much."

"Of course, Stephanie hasn't told you the real reason she wants to go," said Allegra. "She only totally fancies the instructor. Crazy about him."

"Ah yes. The Olympian god of the kitchen. I know."

"Anyway, I think she's silly to look elsewhere when she's got you here. Why go out for a hamburger when you've got beef curry at home?" They grinned as Julian tried to hide his embarrassment. He told them he'd better go back upstairs to finish off his work, and asked if they could please keep the noise down without stifling their creativity?

As he climbed the stairs back up to his box of a study, Julian reflected on what his business (the real one, not this pensions drag) had taught him about human nature. Specifically female nature. What had just gone on in the kitchen was a great illustration of that ancient *ménage a trois:* man, woman and money. He admired financially independent women – they had somehow managed to overcome some particularly stubborn biological tendencies. He also respected those who had almost made it into that category. Like Heather, for example. Surely only bad luck had held her back? But economically self-standing or not, Julian had come to believe, the female of the species ultimately wants a man to provide, to foster that sense of being taken care of, the luxury of being able to slip back into being a little girl every now and then. Probably the very sense of comfort that precedes the desire to become a mother (although in Stephanie's case, business start-ups seemed to be taking the place of children, at least for now). Maybe that was what really separated the Heathers from the

Stephanies of this world? Heather was in a relationship with a policeman, Stephanie with a successful financier. Did it boil down to that? He thought of Rob, and wondered what sort of woman would choose him.

Mid way up the stairs, he stopped, remembering that Stephanie had mentioned Allegra a few months previously. He scratched his head. That's right – she had separated from her husband and was in the process of divorcing him. Maybe not that surprisingly, all things considered. But there was somebody she reminded him of. Straight after graduating from university Julian had managed to find a job at a small heavy engineering firm, roughly a hundred miles outside London. His colleagues had been a friendly, straightforward bunch. Fun too, if you consider drinking beer and talking about cars every night entertaining. The firm had one female employee: a pretty young receptionist with a piercing northern Irish accent. The young engineers would make any excuse to pass by reception to look at her, catch her eye or now and then make an attempt at banter. Julian pictured them adjusting their tie knot and the alignment of the pen clipped into their shirt's top pocket. She had eyes only for the company's owner, an overweight, heavily bearded man in his sixties. Julian had heard rumours of an affair, though most of the time he treated her like an annoying teenager, at least at work. Allegra's pale blue eyes, set wide apart, were a perfect match for hers.

By the time he got to the top of the stairs Julian couldn't stomach the thought of spending another hour in the box room. Pension documentation can wait, he thought; after all it would be months before the financial regulator realised somebody's paperwork was late and began to chase him, initially with polite letters, then with more direct ones in bolder print. He knew the form; it had happened to him before. People who worked for the state always made a lot of noise but carried tiny little sticks.

Julian's parents had wanted him to be government employee, a solid, reliable civil servant. A steady income and job security were, above all, the basis of a good marriage and "family life". He had dutifully applied to Her Majesty's government graduate training programme, but his interview technique had never been good enough to hide his indifference to the careers being offered. He recalled his mother's pleading: "But Jonathan, think of the pension. Nobody will give you security like that. It's worth its weight in gold, can't you see?" Hearing those words in his head, and in particular his mother's tone of voice, Julian was struck by how perfectly his old name suited a boy living at home with his aging parents.

He got dressed quickly and decided to tip toe out silently. The two master chefs would continue to believe he was working as hard as they were. He eased the front door shut so slowly that his arms shook and felt so liberated when he stepped into the breezy Summer morning that he almost ran up the hill to the high street, pausing for half a minute at Café Franz's black painted entrance to stifle a series increasingly deep breaths that were turning into gasps. Suitably becalmed, he walked in and sat down on the corner sofa. He didn't really have much record keeping to do – deleting Heather's name and starting investment was the only administration required – but relished the chance to stretch it out and spend as long as he could in his favourite environment. He ordered a hot chocolate from the most smiling of the young waitresses, inhaled the musty, vaguely sweet air in the café and reached for his smartphone.

He had just opened a text message ("Where are you? – S. x") when *she* walked in. The dark brown bob seemed curled inwards at her shoulders, and one or two strands of slightly lighter brown hair were standing up near the crown of her head. Her chest moved up and down visibly and rapidly but her breathing made no sound. Her mouth was closed. She was doing a superb job of hiding the fact she had been running. From whom? Julian himself had run all the way up here to take a break from domestic harmony, but supposed her reason would be very different. She had brought the large novel with her; at least, it looked like the same one. Julian felt happy that she was settling down to a serious reading session. He imagined the life of an overworked, stressed young student, beset by financial strains and maybe two part-time jobs. Literature was probably her only pleasure.

She was sitting close to Julian at the next table, holding the book open with the cover and spine placed flat on the table. He felt a desperate urge to know what she was reading. Leaning very slightly closer to her, he began to squint at the text. No, no good; it just wasn't clear enough from where he sat. The top line of every page was usually just the book's title in larger letters or italics, but – again, no, too far away. Julian knew it was a matter of being literally two inches nearer. He thought about shifting the position of his rear ever so slightly, but then realised she was looking at him.

She had turned her head by forty-five degrees in one smooth movement, the rest of her body remaining statue like. The milk chocolate eyes were looking at him and the mouth was perfectly expressionless.

"Hh–" Julian took a deep breath and cleared his throat. "Hi!" he said. She nodded once and went back to the book. "So, what are you reading?" he persisted. "That looks like a pretty heavy – I mean, serious book." She rotated the book upwards so it was perpendicular to the table, left it there for one second, nodded again to Julian and went straight back to reading it flat on the table. "Ah, thought so" he said. "Dostoyevsky. You like dark Russian literature, I see."

She shrugged. Then, after what seemed to Julian like several minutes of reading while he looked at her stupidly, she turned to him and said, "Yes. Yes, I do actually. What about you?"

"Absolutely. I love him. Very spiritual. Very… Russian."

"Uh huh." She continued reading. She had her slim fingers wrapped around the top of the book, which remained flat against the formica table top. Julian looked at her small, trimmed, totally functional fingernails and thought of Allegra's flawless crimson manicure.

"I've seen you here a few times," Julian continued. "You're something of a regular?"

"Yes. I suppose I am." The light from the window dimmed momentarily as someone outside walked past, turned around and walked back.

"Are you a student?" asked Julian.

"Yes." Julian looked at her hard and raised his eyebrows, making it clear he expected more of an answer. "Russian and East European studies" she clarified.

"But you're reading that in the English translation."

"Yes, I like to make absolutely sure."

"If there's one thing I've learnt in life, it's to always be as sure as possible. Saves a lot of trouble in the long run."

She smiled, quite sweetly Julian thought; her mouth made a true 'u' shape rather than a line. "So, what do you do?"

"I work in finance. I run an investment fund."

"Well I suppose that requires you to be very sure of what you're doing."

"Yes, that's right. It's pretty hard work, too" Julian said firmly.

"Uh huh. You spend a lot of time in here." Julian couldn't quite make out if she was raising her voice like a question or making a statement. An accusation, perhaps. As it was, her voice was a medium pitched drawl.

"Yes," he acknowledged, "it's a convenient place to catch up on administration. I like to get out of the office. Helps clear my head."

She nodded. "Anyway, I think it's pretty strange."

"What is? What's strange?"

"Investment. The idea that people who've got lots of money want to make more, but without doing any work for it. It's like some kind of conjuring trick. Magic for the wealthy."

"Hmm, you have a point, actually. Never really thought about it that way."

"Not that I've got any money to invest. And if I did, investment wouldn't be high on my list."

"No, I suppose not. What would you do with it?"

"Shopping, no contest. I love shoes."

"Well, so far I've never met a girl who doesn't. What kind of shoes do you like?"

"Expensive ones, of course. And high heels, too. I'm five foot three and need them. But basically expensive."

"Sounds like you've got good taste." Julian looked down at her footwear. She flexed the foot nearer to him up and down at the ankle so he could get a proper viewing: flat sandals, two black straps, one at the ankle, the other over the toes. He saw that her bare heels were badly in need of a pedicure. She realised he had noticed and withdrew her foot quickly.

"Yeah, I know" she said.

So – you study full time? At university?"

"And that's basically why I'm broke. Actually" – she paused – "in fact I do have a job. You could say I work part time." At that instant the light coming through the front window, which had been casting a curious bright rectangle on the girl's right cheek, dimmed almost to the point of extinction. The other customers, who hadn't seemed aware of very much other than their frothy cappuccinos and newspapers, looked up with an air of disappointment, resigning themselves to the certainty that it would be cloudy for the rest of the day.

Julian stared at her now unlit face. Her eyes seemed to be the same shade of brown as her hair. "What do you do?"

"I'm a personal assistant. Sort of. Basically I do secretarial type jobs, run errands for my... my boss. I sometimes deliver things, packages, business papers, you know. The fun part is, I get to accompany his associates to dinners, events, stuff like that. The money can be good sometimes. Depends on the night, really. Men can be strange. Unpredictable." She sighed softly. "Can't say I've saved much, that's for sure."

"Who's your boss? That guy out there in the big coat?" He gestured with his thumb and fist, and as he jabbed back and forth the man's raincoat billowed in and out, as if connected to the tip of Julian's thumb by an invisible string. The girl just looked straight through Julian as if he had said nothing. It occurred to him that this question had been a little too direct; too much, too soon. He would have to wait to find out what was going on between those two.

Julian's face made an expression that said "how stupid of me" and he raised the heel of his hand to his forehead. "Sorry, I should have asked earlier. What is your name? I'm Julian, by the way."

"Well, hello Julian. My name is Sonia."

Sonia. Where had he heard that name before? Then he remembered and pointed at her book. "Sonia. Like in..." He continued to point at the novel in her hand.

She raised her eyebrows and nodded. Julian thought he had finally succeeded in impressing her and that she was determined not to show it. "It's really good to meet you, Sonia. Nice to finally learn your name."

"I thought you weren't interested," she said.

Julian pointed at the book again. "Dostoyevsky wrote a lot about poverty, you know. The sort of desperate acts people are driven to when they lack money."

She thought about that. "I don't think I've done anything too bad. Well, not really desperately bad," she smiled.

"I'm glad to hear that."

"But greed is really the problem. Wanting too much makes you do some terrible things."

Julian tried to nod his head, but found his neck oddly frozen. "Sonia, tell me, do you think we could continue our conversation? Meet up at some point, perhaps?"

"How old are you?" she asked.

"Me? Thirties. In my early thirties. Thirty-three, actually." Arghh. If you want your fib to be convincing, at least sound like you believe it, Julian told himself.

"Right. I see". She turned her head slightly, not to focus on his grey hairs but so she could look out of the window by swivelling her eyes as far as they would go. Her friend in the leather raincoat was now facing sideways. He was staring into the distance and muttering, apparently unconcerned with what was going on inside. "Ok," she said, "I'm going to tell you my phone number, but don't write it down or save it until you're far away from here. Understand?" Julian nodded hard. "O seven nine five three, five o five, six eight three. Got that?" Julian nodded again, squinting upwards and to the left as he recited the number in his head. "Now," she continued, "you're going to get up and leave." She rested her middle fingertip on his knuckle and pressed lightly.

Julian understood perfectly. Without glancing at her again he got up and walked out, manoeuvring around the raincoat man whilst keeping his eyes fixed on the ground. When he was one block away, he quickened his pace to maximum walking speed, which required some concentration to avoid launching into a trot. O seven nine five three, five o five, six eight three. He had a feeling he had just done rather well, despite being very out of practice. That bit about his age. He had done a fine job of keeping a straight face while being both thrilled and amused that she had believed it. Actually – had she? He'd find out soon enough. As he walked, Julian entertained himself by recreating in his head various scenes from his university days. Rob and he had addressed the grand challenge at the centre of human (more specifically male) existence, acquiring female company, by always starting from the point of maximum intoxication, the culmination of that formalised masculine ritual of getting pissed. Alcohol didn't so much give you courage as deaden the pain of rebuffs or the memory of successes, if you could truly call them that. But they were not meeting girls like Sonia back then. O seven nine five three, five o five, six eight three.

What would he do with her? He was a (nearly) married man but certain images persisted in his mind. He would smooth the stray hairs on her head, stroking them down one by one to preserve the symmetry of that brunette bob. He would take her shopping and sit patiently while she tried on a dozen different pairs of heels before choosing the ones that were just right. He would massage her tired feet, pick up her dropped books (even trashy novels), anything that would make her smile and put her arms round him. O seven nine five –

"Julian!" It was a familiar voice, loud, confident and unfriendly. "Talking to yourself, I see. Must say, I knew the day wasn't far off." Julian hadn't realised that the well dressed, middle aged couple he had just walked past were his parents in law. What were they doing here, at the top of the winding high street? It was unusual to see Clive both outside in the open air and walking. Surrounded by neither a domestic interior nor his Mercedes, he gave the impression of a somewhat overweight crab that had decided to go for a crawl without its shell. Kath intervened to explain: "It's been such a strange day, you won't believe it. We thought we'd drop in on you both as a surprise. But then, the car wouldn't start. We had the choice of waiting for three hours for the breakdown service but we just couldn't hang around with weather like this. So we just jumped on the tube. And then, well… we just decided to go for a walk, explore this neck of the woods. Things were getting a little fraught back there."

"Stephanie was in a bit of a state. She really didn't seem very happy and was wondering where you were. What were you up to, Julian?"

"Well, he seems happy," said Kath. "There was a great big smile on his face just then as he was walking up. Better get back home, Julian, and try to cheer her up. Probably the best thing to do right now, don't you think?"

Julian agreed guiltily. "But first," said Clive, pointing behind Julian's right ear, "better say hello to your friend." A second later Julian became aware of the large, dark presence behind him. He turned round. Yes, exactly what he had feared: long leather raincoat, bodybuilder's physique, head shaved almost bald. But this time he looked friendly. He was half smiling, as if the act of looking cheerful was awakening long atrophied muscles in his big square face. He rested a large hand on Julian's shoulder, nodded pleasantly, then walked off. He seemed to be following Julian's exact route home, but striding with an aggression and energy that he felt he'd never duplicate. Julian always walked as if his mind were elsewhere, he realised.

"Curious chap," remarked Clive. "So, can you recommend anywhere decent for a coffee around here? Somewhere on this street, perhaps?"

"Why don't you try Café Franz? Just down here on the right. I know the owner. Some fascinating customers, too." They walked off, down the high street towards the café. Then Julian remembered. "Clive!" he called. No answer. "About that..." and then in a quieter voice, "cheque?" Clive raised his hand vaguely without turning round, as if Julian had said something like "enjoy your walk."

Before walking home, Julian typed Sonia's number into his phone. He thought about the best time to contact her. Maybe in a couple of days' time, with a very non-committal text message? Yes, that would give the right impression. He suddenly remembered the age issue; had she automatically concluded he was married? He was now unable to picture her, the dark hair and small, slender body; even the face, with its constant expression of half puzzlement, half condescension was hard to conjure. He was stuck with an annoying image of a large crustacean.

But he'd have to be careful about leather coat man. Would he be lying in wait for him en route? Julian didn't know whether to walk fast or slow. Eventually he decided to quicken his pace and rush home, gasping slightly half way when he walked past an elderly gentleman in a charcoal grey mackintosh. Opening his front door, he felt both relieved and silly. He walked straight to the kitchen, knowing that's where he would find Stephanie.

She was sitting at the kitchen table, thoughtfully looking down at it. Her face was slightly flushed, as if she'd been crying a few hours ago but had abandoned tears for philosophy and the consolations it might provide. Julian was struck by two things: how tall she was and how beautiful and sorrowful her face looked. "Hi" he said. "What are you doing?"

Her eyes remained fixed on the table top. "It'll never work, that's the problem. I've been trying so hard. All day. It just didn't come together."

"Where's Allegra?"

"She went home. Got bored, I suppose. It wasn't working with the recipes and, well, we didn't see eye to eye on a couple of things."

"Oh dear."

"I should just ditch the whole thing."

"What? Your restaurant idea?"

"Yes. That."

"Come on Stephanie, you can't do that. You've worked so hard."

"Whatever."

"Think of all the effort you've put in. The research. Honestly, I don't know why you give up like this. It's so typical of you. You're really talented. Did you know that?"

"No I'm not." She slowly looked up at him.

"Look, you are talented. I know that, even if you don't"

"I think you're trying to butter me up, that's all. Where have you been, anyway?"

"Where have *I* been?"

"Yes, you – who else? Seriously, I really have no idea what you're doing these days. Why are you always disappearing?"

Julian walked over to her. He put his hand on hers, squeezed it and then picked it up. Her arm remained floppy; her hand wanted to stay on the table. Smiling cheekily, he tried pulling it, trying to make her get up, but she sat firm and pouted her lips, even though her eyes had started to smile. "Come on," he said. A small shake of her head told him he wasn't going to get his way so easily.

"So why don't you explain."

"What?"

"Why you think I'm talented."

"You're talented because you're creative. You try, you create, and that's more important than getting the result you expect. Or what other people expect from you."

"Sometimes I just create a mess"

"That's what I do a lot of the time. I just look like I know what I'm doing."

"Yes, but you're – *successful*." She emphasised the word that excused everything, especially the actions required to achieve it. Julian looked at the floor. "Why so serious?" she asked.

"You're right." He looked up suddenly and smiled his broad, little boy smile. He'd been keeping that in reserve for weeks. "No need to be sombre." He took her hand, squeezed it and pulled. This time there was no resistance.

Chapter 4

It was hours before his alarm clock was due to go off, but Julian found himself awake and lying perfectly still. The early summer night was on the verge of changing from navy to grey blue. What time was it – 4am, perhaps? He couldn't be bothered to roll over, stretch and find out. He felt perfectly rested, as if he'd just had a full night's sleep. His mind was alert, and he thought hard about whether there was something he should be worrying about – a slip up he'd made somewhere, a word too many to the wrong person? But no, he could think of nothing. He was simply enjoying lying there.

He looked next to him where Stephanie was sleeping. She had the covers pulled up to the base of her skull and was lying on her front, slightly curled up. Her face was completely hidden and only her hair seemed to move up and down, as if a uniform mass, as she breathed. He spent a minute or two looking at her, allowing himself the luxury of thinking that everything was all right in his life.

Stretching an arm out for his blue silk dressing gown, he decided to get up and walk around quietly. Perhaps that might make him tired enough to want to go back to bed. He thought he should take an early look at his emails: the internet provided perpetual distraction for alert, unoccupied minds. He located his smartphone and picked it up, causing it to flare up in a multiple ringed aura of bluish white light. He scowled and put it down gently. Walking over to the bedroom door, he pushed it open as slowly as he had the patience to. He walked downstairs and then towards the front door, as if about to leave for one of his head clearing strolls. Lying face down on the doormat was a grey rectangular envelope, the normal size for a letter. He picked it up. It was surprisingly heavy and its surface, although smooth to look at, was richly textured to the touch. He put it in one of the large lower pockets of his dressing gown and climbed the stairs. Entering the bedroom, he lay down, inhaled deeply and closed his eyes.

When he woke up again the bedroom was lit up brightly with nine o'clock sunshine streaming through the maple blinds, partially blocked off by Stephanie's head. She was sitting astride him, one bare leg either side of the dressing gown, stretching the silk belt tightly over his abdomen. He took rapid, shallow breaths.

".. Considerable talent. A money manager of considerable talent." She was reading from the letter, holding it in one hand whilst clutching the ripped open envelope in the other. "Julian, fancy that. Someone thinks you're talented!"

"Hmm? Er... good morning. What did you say just then?"

"This. The letter you've just got. I must say this stationery is gorgeous. What a lovely shade of pale green! With a touch of olive, too."

"Olive? Julian took the letter. Both his mouth and eyes were dry. He blinked several times and then swallowed, expecting his body to produce moisture where required. Squinting, and with a very sceptical expression on his face, Julian started to read the old fashioned monospaced type:

Dear Mr Julian Kay,

It has come to my attention that you are a financial advisor and money manager of considerable talent. I have been made aware of the superior investment results that you have been able to generate.

In this age of false marketing and salesmen posing as experts, true talent is something to be valued. I am an entrepreneur of several decades' experience and have funds to invest.

I would appreciate a meeting with you. Please come to visit me at No. 22 Hogarth Road (I believe we are practically neighbours) at your convenience.

Yours sincerely,
Richard R. Stein

Julian sat up, pushing Stephanie as she rolled off him. Well. What an odd letter. Although Julian certainly didn't mind being called talented. Is this a joke, he wondered? If so, then someone must have gone to quite a bit of expense with that letter paper. But not providing any contact details other than a street address was unusual. Then again, it was just up the hill. A five minute walk would be all it would take to find out if the joke really was on him.

"Everything all right?" asked Stephanie.

"Oh yeah, sure. Someone's interested in investing." He brandished the folded up letter. "This really makes a change from the usual emails. Looks pretty classy. He might be what we in the business call a high net worth client". He smiled, and Stephanie took her turn to push him back down onto the bed. "Anyway, better find out what it's all about."

"When are you going to go?"

Julian thought for a few seconds and said "I wouldn't mind going up there today actually. There's nothing you need me for, is there, particularly?"

"No, not today," she replied. "Well, I'll leave you to it. Hang on – which road is it again?" She took the letter and skimmed it. "Ah, Hogarth Road. Thought so. That's where all those massive–"

"Yes, that's the one".

"Well, good luck! That's all I can say. Don't be gone too long, eh?"

Julian said "no" quietly and shook his head. Right – he needed to get dressed. Stephanie got up, threw on her half-length dressing gown and skipped downstairs. Julian thought he should dress especially well for this Mr Stein he was about to meet. Somehow his clothes had to be in the same bracket as that stationery. He knew his usual department store suits simply wouldn't do. Luckily, he had something in reserve. A suit that until now had remained unworn outside the confines of his bedroom: his first and only fully bespoke Savile Row suit, an extravagance he once thought he would never come close to indulging in. He had had it made as soon as his first client had joined the scheme, convinced it – and similar ones yet to be tailored – would help propel him into the wealthiest social groups. He had never actually felt comfortable wearing it but today he was determined to break it in, to make it part of his skin. Today was special.

He first put on an ivory shirt, fastened all the buttons up to the top and slid in a pair of steel collar stays. He chose a red spotted tie, which he did up in a half Windsor knot, then put on the two-piece grey herringbone suit. It felt quite uncomfortable – somewhat tight around the shoulders – but he couldn't stop admiring himself in the mirror. He flexed and rotated his shoulders a little and after a minute or two, it was as if the suit were not there. A pair of dark chocolate brown Oxfords (along with a matching briefcase) completed the look.

As he walked up the hill to Hogarth Road, Julian felt elated, excited in a way he hadn't felt since the early days of the scheme. He recalled the feeling of having that first cheque hit his bank account, the delight at the handful of small luxuries that had finally been purchased after a long delay. Hogarth Road was a familiar turning on his left and, as at every other time he had made it, his breathing became faster and shallower as soon as the huge houses came into view. No. 22 was very slightly smaller than its neighbours but architecturally far more pleasing, having the appearance of a Lutyens. There were a few cars scattered around the driveway, mainly of the Volvo-esque, utilitarian type, but parked slightly further away from the main group was a rather handsome vintage sports car. The week end getaway car, thought Julian.

He stood up straight and knocked loudly on the door. Then he saw an ornate brass door knocker, situated just off to the side. He knocked loudly again, the correct way. "Yes, one moment!" called a man's voice. Twenty seconds or so later, the door swung open and the same voice said, very matter-of-factly, "Hello. Can I help you?" He was a shade over six feet tall, straight and wiry, except for the beginnings of a small paunch. Grey haired – cut short at the back and sides, slicked back on top - and probably around sixty years old, he had a distinct ex-military look. He wore brown tweed trousers and a slim fitting white shirt – an older man's rather formal get up for relaxing at home. The vowels were rounded, middle class but not plummy. Retired army officer, Julian instantly judged. So pleased was he with this assessment that he forgot to say anything. The man raised his eyebrows and smiled.

"Good morning. I'm looking for Richard Stein. Does he live here?"

"I am Richard Stein. What is it that I can I do for you?"

"Ah, well." Julian cleared his throat. "It may actually be more a case of what I could do for you. Er..." Richard Stein looked blank. "I'm Julian Kay. You wrote me a letter?"

"Ah, yes!" Stein's sharp featured face lit up with warmth and recognition. He had quite a pleasant smile. "Of course. Do come in. I'm surprised you managed to make it over here quite so soon. Thank you." Julian hesitated for a second, and Stein said "Come on in!" holding the door wide open for him. "You may have noticed this house looks a little different from the others. It's an original from the 1920s. The others are a bit more – *recent*, you might say. Have you heard of Herbert Baker?" Julian told him the name rang a bell. "A close associate of Edwin Lutyens. This is one of the very small number of English suburban houses he designed." He led Julian through a sparsely furnished, musty smelling marble floored hallway into a large and truly gorgeous living room: dark tan carpets, macassar and cream leather furniture. Julian walked towards the long sofa in the centre – allowing Stein to take a good look at his suit – and sat down at one end, right on the edge, putting his briefcase down by his feet. Stein hitched his trousers up before sitting down on an armchair and crossing his legs. "Firstly," he said, "Can I get you anything? Tea, coffee, some wine perhaps?" Julian shook his head. Stein put his fingertips together. "Now" he said, "Let's talk money."

"Okay," Julian started off a little hoarsely. "I suppose a good starting point would be to discuss what you're trying to achieve financially. Your goals." He stopped, looked around at the sumptuous room and decided that there really wasn't any need to talk about financial goals. "Or rather, let me start by asking you a question. What made you get in touch with me?"

Stein looked hard at Julian. "I simply recognised a fellow businessman. That's all, really."

"Right" said Julian, struggling not to look confused.

"Not a salesman, nor a timewaster or so called advisor. Or even worse, an 'expert'. Basically, not a complete and utter bullshitter, if you'll excuse my language." His accent had changed. The middle class diction had faded to reveal a cockney tonal base.

"Ok. Thanks." Julian shifted his position slightly on the sofa.

"The point is," Stein continued in his posher voice, "I've had a lot of people work for me over the years. Not all of them have been particularly capable. Or even competent, for that matter."

"I see," said Julian.

"But, what can you do? Apart from get rid of them, of course. Harder if they've been with you for a long time, though."

"I'm sure that can cause problems. So tell me, Mr Stein, which business are you in exactly?"

"Nightclubs. A few media investments too, but generally it's nightlife and casinos." The corners of his mouth turned up, but the eyes didn't smile. "Which is sort of indirectly how I got to know about you."

"Really?" Julian's eyes widened.

"Yes, your favourite watering hole. What's it called, Westway House? Yes, that's it. Used to own a small share in it. I visited once or twice and there was quite a bit of a – buzz, shall we say – about you. The smart clothes, those elegant cocktails, that professional reserve. It all made quite an impression."

"Gosh. Well, that's good to know, I suppose."

So, I sent over one of my guys to check you out. Julian raised his eyebrows. Exactly who had Stein sent to investigate him? Stein puffed out his cheeks and put on a whiny, rather over earnest voice: "I'm an accountant, you know, my clients pay me to be cautious".

Julian could not move for a couple of seconds. His arms and legs tingled. "My God, that's brilliant. Uncanny. Paul Kelmer! You've got quite a talent for impersonations, Mr Stein."

"Good old Paul. Reliable chap. Not really the sharpest brain I've got working for me but, as I say, trustworthy." Stein's face darkened, in a way that Julian had somehow been expecting from the moment he had met him. "Listen, I think we can get straight to the point, Julian. I know what you've been doing. I've been in business an awful long time and I believe I can read people." Julian sat perfectly still. "These investment profits you've been making. Phenomenal. I mean, they are unbelievably good. Do you think I haven't worked out what you're up to?"

Julian tried not to look nervous. He fixed his eyes on a large, square grey marble ashtray. "What... do you think I'm up to?"

"Well, I'm not sure *exactly* what it is you're doing, but there is one thing I do know. It's illegal, right? Something like insider trading or whatever. Can't say

I'm much of a finance expert but I know crooked when I see it."

Instantly Julian felt more annoyed than nervous. Who the hell did this Mr Stein think he was? Inviting him home to call him a criminal? "Now, look here," he said firmly.

But Stein had started smiling. "Relax, my friend, take it easy. I'm not going to tell on you! No, you completely misunderstand. I was actually paying you a compliment. All my life I've been surrounded by the weak and stupid. Incompetent at best. It has hindered my career and cost me money. A lot of money. And finally, I come across someone like you. Someone with vision. Someone who actually gets things done, produces results, and is clever enough not to trip up. Not some fool who cannot pull his head out of the rulebook."

"I see," said Julian. "Well, thanks. I think."

"You're welcome. Very welcome, Julian. And now, before you think you've wasted your time and that super new suit coming up here, well, I have something I'd like to tell you. I'd like to invest. Yes, something fairly substantial. Something around the seven figure mark. How does that sound?"

Julian tried not to look excited. "Sure, that would be a good amount. To start with, I mean. So, you'd definitely like to go ahead?"

"Just tell me the account name, number and sort code. The famous trio. I'll be able to wire you the funds this afternoon. There isn't much in the way of paperwork, I assume?"

Julian thought quickly. He didn't want such a large amount of money hitting the account all at once. Seven figures would be five times the largest investment he had received so far, and of course the bank would start asking questions. Now of course, he could ask Stein for a smaller amount. But everything about him hated that idea. He looked around at that splendid drawing room once more. No, that wasn't going to happen. Julian knew what he had to do: start using the numbered Swiss bank account he had set up years ago and not touched at all since its inception. "Actually, Mr Stein, could you write me out a cheque? I'm not fully set up yet for electronic transfers. I am working on it, though." That's the thing about anonymous accounts: international banking law prevents them from being part of any electronic payment system.

Stein shrugged. "All right" he said. "Let me get my chequebook. It's in my study." He walked out of the room leisurely. Julian stood up and started looking around as soon as Stein was out of earshot. His attention was drawn by the hi-fi system on the other side of the room. It was some obscure English make that Julian had vaguely heard of – very exclusive and highly regarded. He looked around at Stein's music collection. Lots of classical CDs, several jazz. He longed to hear them being played: the highest musical fidelity in the most impressive house he'd ever been invited to. But that was for another time. He sat down quickly and Stein reappeared a few seconds later. "Here we are," said Stein after scribbling out the cheque in black ballpoint. Julian looked at it (yes, it was seven figures) and put it in the inside right pocket of his suit jacket. Stein almost had his hand on Julian's shoulder as they walked back to the front door. Julian couldn't help feeling he had just made a new friend. He sensed they'd be seeing a lot more of each other, that they'd grow close over time. "Goodbye, Julian, and good luck" said Stein at the door, shaking Julian's hand. "And please" – here a little smile appeared, a genuine one – "don't let me down. You really wouldn't want to do that!"

Julian wanted to rush home to admire the cheque. Play with it, fondle it. Inhale the aroma of the stiff paper. He felt like a child. Stein had had that effect on him, subjecting him to a test that he had presumably passed. For now, at least. He walked around the incongruously humdrum family saloons in the driveway and noticed that the sports car – that vintage beauty – had moved, and was now parked a few metres away on the street. As he got closer to it he saw a dark haired man sitting inside; closer still and he saw the grey hairs. The man got out. "Hello, Julian. How's business these days?"

"Hi. Wow, Toby, good to see you. How are you?"

Toby nodded slightly. "Still at it. Doing my best. I see you know Mr Stein." He jerked his thumb towards the house. "Social visit, was it?"

"Actually it was business. Mr Stein… uh, he was thinking about investing in my fund."

"And?"

"Well, he's mulling it over. I explained how it works and left him with some information. I guess he'll get back to me when he's decided one way or the other."

Julian scratched his chest, just above the inside right pocket.

Toby nodded, slowly and deliberately, and said "ah" voicelessly. "Tell me, Julian. Do you run any background checks on your customers?"

"Nothing beyond the usual. You know, proof of address, passport, that sort of thing."

"Right. If you have a few minutes, Julian, could we go for a short drive? There's something I really need to talk to you about." Julian hesitated but couldn't think of a decent excuse. "Literally, just a few minutes. I don't want to go into details right here."

Julian gave in. "I suppose a few minutes wouldn't hurt." Damn. He wanted to get that beautiful cheque out of this tight suit and into a safe place. Like under his pillow. "Do you fancy just driving around this neighbourhood for a while? The weather's quite nice and the houses are beautiful. As you well know by now." Toby nodded once in agreement. Julian folded himself up and squeezed into the passenger seat of the Porsche. The engine began its enraged phut-phutting and he recalled the night Toby had given him a lift home. Jolting forward as Toby accelerated away from the house, Julian immediately realised why fast cars were so seductive: being thrown around physically, that violent lurching and instability generated fear, the emotion that always makes everything else seem so real. Perhaps it was time for Julian to buy one. After all, things were looking up on the financial front. "So what did you want to talk about, Toby?"

"I wanted to tell you a bit about Richard Stein. Before you get in over your head."

"Over my head? What do you mean?"

"Listen, mate, I need to talk to you as a friend as well as a member of the police force. Normally we don't talk about our work to members of the public, but I'm making an exception here. Stein is currently under investigation."

"I think I understand why you're talking to me. Warning me off before he becomes a client. Is that it?"

"Pretty much. He has a long criminal past. And a very promising future, too, I'll bet. We've been struggling to gather evidence. Some undeclared income was the worst we found."

Julian considered having at least some hidden income more of a social duty than a crime. He could never understand why the government needed to take quite so much of people's money. "I see. What's he supposed to have done?"

"Drugs. Possibly ordered an execution or two, but he's definitely made a fortune from drug running." The word 'running' coincided with a sharp, roaring swerve. They had just turned into a street of very slightly more modest houses. "The key problem is all our information is anecdotal. People have spoken to us, off the record, but we just don't have any solid evidence."

Julian kept a straight face. "Has he killed anyone? Do you know for sure?"

"Not with his own hands. But if he wants someone gone, you can be pretty sure that individual will have a somewhat curtailed life expectancy. Things just seem to work out that way." All right, thought Julian. No concrete evidence. He really can't have done anything that bad. A bit of drug pushing – wasn't that just satisfying a demand? "It's the way he puts everything through his books," continued Toby. "Masterful. With his network of clubs and restaurants, and all those temporary workers coming and going, well, we don't know quite where to start." Julian smiled inwardly. Yes, he did sound pretty clever. "So what I really need to tell you, Julian, is please – for your own sake, if no one else's – stay away from Richard Stein and his money. You really don't want him as a client."

"No. You're right. If he chooses to go ahead I'll make up some excuse or another and turn him down. I'm not sure he will anyway." Julian's left hand began to wander towards the inside pocket. He stopped it before it got there.

"Well, it's up to you. As I said, we have nothing solid on him. It's actually a bit of an obsession of mine, coming up here and lurking outside his house. I've almost become one of the local residents. By the way, how did he find out about your investment fund? Did you approach him directly?"

"My father in law uses the same accountant. I suppose he must've put in a good word for me."

"Right. Interesting connection there."

"Yes indeed. So, Toby, tell me – how are you getting along with Heather? Have you two moved into your new place yet?"

"Yes we have, as a matter of fact. It's really smart. Much bigger than we thought we'd be able to afford. I guess we just got lucky, eh? Or maybe London property is hitting a soft patch, who knows. Anyway, we'd love to invite you and – Stephanie, isn't it? – round for dinner some time. Let me know when you can make it."

"That sounds great. I'll hold you to it! So, is Heather happy with everything? Has she had a chance to get the interior decoration up to scratch? I know she can be a little particular."

Toby laughed. "You know her pretty well. I forgot how far back you two go. Yes, particular is a nice word for it. High maintenance, some would say. Not me, but some people. I've spent the last couple of weeks being dragged round more than my fair share of designer furniture shops. Oh yeah, not to mention the three hours per day that I've been assigned to the internet. My mission is to find precisely the right tiles for the kitchen and bathroom." He stopped for air. "Personally, I quite liked it the way it was when we moved in. Nice and plain. But what does that matter?" He was grinning.

"I sympathise. I really do. Toby, any further thoughts regarding–"

"The investment? Sure, to be honest I can't stop thinking about your fund and all the money it's making. Really, especially at the moment. I could use some extra regular income right now, believe me. I knew moving would be expensive but, what with the deposit, the decorating, Helen's high standards, well, you know. I just can't seem to get the cash together. If only. By the way, what's the minimum amount to buy in? I suppose you'd need a good couple of grand at least?"

Julian hesitated. "Actually, the starting minimum is twenty-five thousand pounds."

Toby looked startled, then angry. He accelerated sharply, causing Julian to grip the seat with both hands and regret what he had just told him. Toby waited a few seconds, then, apparently calmer, said in a soft voice, "Twenty-five thousand quid? Where does an average bloke or girl get that sort of money from? But yes, I know what sort of customers you want. City types. Family money. Oh well, my meagre savings aren't going to get me too far, that's for sure. Hey, well, I knew there was going to be a catch. You've got to be rich to get in in the first place!"

Julian realised that Toby, on the verge of becoming a (potentially very useful) friend, felt alienated, excluded from a club he thought he was about to gain admittance to. Just the mention of that sum of money had seemed like a smack in the face to him. Julian had had a similar experience at university. He had made friends with a group of students – two men and a woman on the same engineering course as him – who were as keen on literature and architecture as he was. Following months of getting to know one another over coffee and smoke fuelled late night discussions and trips to museums, they had decided to plan a week long holiday in Florence. Julian had been thrilled. But when he discovered that instead of youth hostels they had intended to stay at a smart hotel, and generally do everything in a style he aspired to but could not afford, he made an excuse and dropped out. The intensity of that particular friendship seemed to subside from that point onwards, changing from intimacy to casual warmth, then friendliness and in the end only politeness. After leaving university they had not kept in touch with him. If only they could see him now. He could pay for everyone to go to Florence and stay in a suite overlooking the Duomo.

"Actually," said Toby thoughtfully, "this car cost me twenty-five grand. But all it does is drain my cash. Thousands every year. Ironic, isn't it?"

"Toby, look, it's not set in stone. I might be able to reduce the initial deposit you need to stump up. I can't guarantee anything, but really, I'm going to look into ways to make it more flexible."

Toby didn't say anything but attempted to look grateful. The journey home seemed more subdued, the engine less angry, humbled by reality as much as its driver had just been. Julian directed Toby to his house and they stopped just outside. Toby took Julian's hand and clasped it, thumbs interlocking. His eyes appeared watery. Looking earnestly at Julian, he said "I think you're doing a great job and wish you all the best. Be careful, my friend, and stay safe." Julian got out of the car and walked towards his front door without saying anything. As Toby was driving off, Julian carefully felt the contents of his top right inner jacket pocket with his left hand. Yes, the cheque was safe and so, for the time being, was his scheme and way of life. He wondered what Stephanie had been doing with her day.

He felt tired, completely drained. It was only mid-afternoon but a full day of surprises had come and gone. He began to yawn, a series of rapid, very deep, cleansing yawns. A doctor had told him years ago that the evolutionary function of yawning was to keep an exhausted human body awake for a few more vital minutes. It could be the difference between life and death. He shut the front door and walked to the foot of the stairs.

"Sleepyhead!" Stephanie called to him. Julian turned round and saw that she was dressed for a day spent in town. She was wearing her high heels (which made her look especially tall) and navy beret. "Make sure you don't fall asleep in that suit. That really would be a shame."

"What did you get up to today?" Julian just about managed to ask.

"Shopping," she replied. "And wouldn't you like to know what I bought."

"What's that?" he yawned.

"Well, I happened to be on Bond Street today, you know, just strolling, window shopping. Not really intending to buy anything. In fact, I had made up my mind not to spend any money today." Julian started climbing the stairs. "But then I walked past Bodleys – they are literally slap bang in the middle of Bond Street – and you know I just can't resist the beautiful things they've got. I mean, normally I'd just walk past, but then I saw this." She held up a sheaf of about fifty sheets of luxury writing paper loosely tied up with a pale gold ribbon. The paper was half way between pale and military green. "This really reminded me of that letter we got this morning. The colour's a bit more girly though, don't you think?" Julian looked down. It was, but rather nice nonetheless. "You know, I really want to write something. A recipe, perhaps." When he got to the bedroom, Julian took off his suit jacket and lay down on the bed. He had left the cheque in the inside pocket which, bearing in mind the events of the day, was probably the safest place for it. "Don't forget about tomorrow!" was the last thing he heard before he dozed off. "The taxi's booked for eleven o'clock in the morning".

Chapter 5

Julian sat at his desk in the spare box room that he had
months ago christened his study. The bottom edge of the
cheque rested on the part leather surface of the desk
while he held it upright, one finger and thumb each side.
He stared at it. In a few minutes it would put into a bog
standard envelope and couriered off to Geneva, to be
processed, transacted on, scanned and ultimately burnt
or shredded. It deserved more attention: the stiff pale
tan watermarked paper, the carelessly scrawled
numerals that made up the seven-digit figure and the
curiously childish looking signature at the bottom right
hand corner were all things to be savoured. Julian loved
cheques. They had a physical, sensual reality. This one
in particular meant he wouldn't need to do any more
pensions administration. How odd that one man's

destiny could be changed by a few casual strokes of a more powerful man's pen.

He remembered his first ever attempt at fraud. He was thirteen years old. He and a classmate, a good friend named Niall, had, out of the blue, become obsessed with plastic self-assembly model aircraft (the obsession later passed just as suddenly). Their desire to build exceeded their ability to purchase, so to enhance the economic power of their weekly allowance and odd scraps of earned money, they had decided on a ruse: price tag swapping. Julian had provided the distraction, quizzing the shopkeeper in depth about the relative merits of enamel versus acrylic paints. Meanwhile, the manually dextrous Niall had peeled off the price stickers of a large scale bomber and scaled down first world war biplane. Swapping them around and re-sticking them, the boys had managed to acquire a prestigious model at a quarter its real price. The puzzled expression on the aged shopkeeper's face, as he tried to work out how such a gross pricing error had occurred, had terrified Julian. He had felt sure he was on the verge of being caught: humiliated, made to look a fool and given a serious talking to by the cops. He would be expelled from school and never gain admission to a good university. He had had a full scale asthma attack as soon as they had made it out of the shop, undetected. They had got away with it, but his respiratory system hadn't been convinced. Julian leaned back in the chair and laughed aloud. The terror of crime no longer plagued him. Today it was a simple matter of logistics, minimising administration, warding off the curious. How to make fraud as profitable and hassle free as possible: that was the only real challenge left.

"Julian, can you be a hero and help us with our bags?" Hearing Allegra's musical voice call for him from downstairs reminded him which day it was. She and Stephanie were off for their week long residential course. Out in the country somewhere – Hampshire, Julian vaguely remembered Stephanie saying – a group of keen amateur chefs would be perfecting their kitchen technique and learning the management skills required to run their own restaurant. The female attendees would, of course, have the added pleasure of personal tuition from the handsome instructor. Julian felt relieved that for one week he would not be the centre of attention. What would he do with this window of freedom? He walked down the stairs and saw both women dressed in summer outfits: flowery print culottes, strappy sandals and loose tops. "So where's the taxi parked?" he asked, peering out of the window adjoining the front door. Grabbing both small suitcases, he put them in the boot of the cab and said goodbye, kissing both women (Allegra only on the cheek, though slightly too close to the corner of her mouth for comfort).

Right – that cheque. There really had been far too much lingering. Back in his study he printed off a covering letter, folded it up with the cheque and stuffed both into a white envelope. On his way to the local courier pick up office he walked past George McCrum. "Looking busy, Julian. Glad to see it!" he called out as Julian sped past him. "You've got a lot to smile about, I'll say." Julian self-consciously pursed his lips to get rid of the stray smile, carried out his business with the courier and rushed back to his study, panting just a little.

He got out his smartphone and hit several keys on the screen's pop up keypad in quick succession, as if he'd been practising the entire sequence as a single move. He had actually typed out the full name (S, o, n, i, a) when just the "s" and the "o" would have sufficed. He thought of a good message. Interesting, non-committal. He cleared his throat and started to type: "Hi Sonia, how's things? Could meet today if you want. Julian." He immediately regretted that. It sounded like a clumsy young man: studiedly casual, which is the worst way of being unoriginal. He thought he'd give it one more attempt. He waited ten minutes. Then he stretched it out to fifteen. All right, there hadn't been an answer, so he tried: "Sonia, fancy meeting up for some shopping? Shoes, I was thinking. J."

The answer came back in under ten seconds, as if he had contacted some electronic device providing automated responses. "Hi Julian, that sounds really great. Where and when do you want to meet?"

"How about the high street? There are some good shops around there. Meet you just outside Café Franz in half an hour?"

"Sounds cool," she texted back. "See you soon! X"

He kept his pale blue jeans on but exchanged the trainers for a pair of tasselled brown loafers. He made sure he arrived a full ten minutes early, withdrew cash from a nearby ATM and stood slouching at the entrance to the café. Changing his posture every now and then, he kept one eye on the coffee sippers and muffin nibblers sitting outside and the other on the street. A quarter of an hour after arriving he saw a pair of figures in the distance, very close but not touching, walking towards him. It was a tall man and a petite girl with short hair. Argh, she's brought him along, Julian thought. Great. He stood straighter, sighed, and waited. Two minutes later Sonia and her tall friend, still in a raincoat but this time a lighter coloured one, were standing opposite him. Julian smiled at Sonia and she winked at him. He was about to introduce himself to raincoat man and held out a hand, but Sonia's companion just tightened his mouth, nodded and turned round sharply. He then walked off as if he had no idea who either Julian or Sonia were. "Hi. Sonia. How are you?" Julian asked earnestly.

"Fine, thank you, sir." She was looking up at him from under her fringe. Her large hazel eyes were perfectly clear, almost shining. In her tight black jeans and white t-shirt she looked adorable. For a girl who never smiled, that is.

"So, no novel today?" Julian grinned.

"You can't read every day. Not when you've got better things to do. Like today, obviously."

"Indeed. Just – tell me something. Who is that guy? I've seen him with you a few times. You two seem very close."

"Well. We're friends. He's actually my ex-boyfriend, but that really was ages ago. Nowadays we just hang out. It's working out really well. For a friendship, I mean."

"I... see."

"Look, it isn't what it looks like. He's just a friend. I told him I was going to do some shopping with you and he walked me up here. He wanted to make sure everything was okay. No harm in that, is there?"

"Well it's good you've got someone to look out for you."

"Yes, and he does. He often picks me up after work, you know, if it's late."

"When you're entertaining?"

She nodded and her glossy dark bob shimmered. "So." She put her palms together. "Where are we going shopping?"

"The lady doth require shoes," said Julian "and I know the finest local purveyor." He held out his hand and Sonia held it, giggling. The shop that Julian had in mind (he had walked past it hundreds of times) was tiny, a specialist boutique stocking essentially two types of footwear: glamorous high heeled shoes and glamorous *very* high heeled shoes. Sonia's face looked thrilled as she peered inside. "As I remember, heels were what you said you needed?"

She nodded hard. "So, are you coming inside with me? While I try them on?"

"No," Julian said quickly, "I'll wait out here. You go in and buy them." He opened his wallet and counted out £300. He handed the cash to her. "Looks like that's your budget. Enjoy." She folded the bundle of notes and put it in the front pocket of her jeans. She took one last look at Julian and went inside.

Julian was at a loose end. He walked around in small circles outside the shop, first clockwise, then twice more anticlockwise, staring at the tassels on his loafers. It occurred to him that he had never bought any clothes or shoes for Stephanie, nor taken her shopping. She had always done that sort of thing alone or with her friends, using money she had earned or been given by her parents. Thus far Julian had been spared this classic feeling of male redundancy. He stopped circling for a moment and decided to look, discreetly, into the shop through the front window. The sun was shining on the glass and he had to blink and refocus a couple of times before he could see anything other than his own reflection. Ah, yes, Sonia was sitting down with a large array of shoes with their boxes scattered around her. A shop assistant, a girl roughly her own age but much taller, was giving her her full attention. Julian turned round before either of them had a chance to look up.

"You look like a man waiting for his better half. You've just got that look about you, Julian." It was George McCrum, whose late morning walk had today, for some reason, taken him right past the very place Julian really shouldn't have been. "Don't worry, I'm sure she won't be all day."

"I hope not," Julian answered, turning his head round to the window very slightly. "How have you been, George? Did you walk all the way up here?"

"I did, something I'm proud of still being able to do, hey hey." He looked as if he had just remembered something, and raised his index finger. "Listen, Julian – about this investment fund of yours."

"Yes?" McCrum had been a tough sell in the first place. What did he want to know now?

"Well, I'm still as thrilled as ever with the money we've been making. But I was reading in – the Financial Times, was it, or maybe the Sunday business section, I can't quite remember – well, things are looking a bit uncertain in the financial world right now."

"In what way?"

"It's just that we might be on the verge of a recession. What do you think?"

"George, the frank answer is, I don't know, and nor does anyone else. Are you worried about anything?"

"Well, yes, to be honest. What if something goes wrong in the stock market? Are we still going to be able to keep making the profits?"

"George, it doesn't matter what the stock market does or doesn't do. We make money whether it goes up, down or sideways."

"Ok, but what about the foreign exchange market? Sterling could crash any time."

"Our algorithms make money either way, whatever happens. Remember?"

"Ok, right. Yes, I think I got that when you explained it to me the first time." He still looked concerned. He stood still, apparently with no intention of continuing his stroll.

Julian came up and stood close to him. He hadn't realised how short McCrum was; he seemed to have shrunk since their last meeting. "Look, if something's troubling you, I'd be very happy to come over and chat to you sometime. Okay?" McCrum nodded but was still standing fast. It wasn't yet time to continue his walk. Julian put his hand lightly on his shoulder. "Honestly, Mr

McCrum, whenever's convenient." With something half way between a reassuring pat and a shove, Julian pushed McCrum forward, a movement which soon became a shuffle and, after a couple of seconds' acceleration, eventually turned into the rest of his afternoon stroll. "Enjoy your walk, Mr McCrum, the weather's beautiful." The expression on McCrum's face was that of someone pretending to understand something solely to avoid yet another incomprehensible explanation.

Julian stared at the back of his grey head as he walked away.

This sort of thing – potentially embarrassing situations in public – should not be happening. Julian resolved never again to be so vulnerable, to not loiter when difficult clients were in the vicinity. What was wrong with them? They had been lucky to be allowed to invest in the first place, after all. Any concerns and they should email or write like civilised people. No, chaps like Marek the builder and Sunil his dentist were the type of customer Julian wanted. They had been genuinely thankful for being allowed on board. Sunil just let him get on with it – "I'll keep making the money, you keep growing it for me" – and Marek, once he had managed to get his modest starting deposit together, had felt thrilled to be in on such an exclusive opportunity, convinced that life in this new country was only going to get better for him.

Julian turned round. Sonia was standing in the shop's doorway (how long had she been there?) looking her usual intense little self except for the fact that she had grown six inches. She was wearing her new shoes, a pair of dark red stilettos. Julian thought of a small girl trying on her mother's shoes, then immediately tried to banish the thought from his mind. "And look at you," he said. "I'm going to have to get used to Tall Sonia. The new version." She laughed.

"Thank you, Julian," she said and gave him a brief hug. "By the way, I got something for you, too." She opened the carrier bag which held her old pair of shoes in the box belonging to the new shoes. She pulled out a small, slim patent leather black wallet. It was elegant, understated.

Julian was thrilled. It looked expensive and he was touched that Sonia had used part of her budget for him. "Thank you. Wow. I'm surprised you had enough money left to buy me something like that."

"Well..." She was biting her lower lip forcefully with her front teeth showing. She shifted her weight from one foot to the other.

"What?" Julian smiled.

"I didn't actually buy it. It was just lying there on the shelf, not doing very much and I, well, sort of swiped it. But you like it. That's the important thing."

For one fleeting moment Julian felt thrilled, but that rapidly gave way to shock. "What? Are you completely crazy? I take you shopping so you – you decide to do some thieving for good measure? I mean, you are totally–" He stopped himself, rather taken aback at his own hypocrisy.

She looked at him, unmoving. She appeared neither angry nor contrite. Nor particularly scared at just having been accused of theft. "Anything else?" she said.

"How can anyone do something like that?" Julian had intended the question to be rhetorical, but it came out sounding like he actually wanted to know.

"You mean technically, or morally?"

"Both, I suppose."

"Being a customer is the perfect cover for anyone who wants to steal," she explained. "Whilst you're trying on different pairs of shoes and ordering the sales assistant around, keeping her busy, you've got the perfect opportunity to grab something. No one suspects anything because you're the customer. You are actually there to spend money."

"Yes, that makes sense. You, the customer at an expensive shop, are someone important. You are in a position of power, of prestige. Therefore, the idea of you committing a crime is completely below anyone's radar." A crafty smile grew on Julian's face. "I like it."

"I thought you'd appreciate the logic, at least," said Sonia.

"Right. So that's the how part out of the way. Now tell me why you do it."

Sonia appeared to be thinking deeply. She had breezed through the first part of the answer but now looked genuinely at a loss. "I suppose it's because…" She stopped and thought some more. "No, I'll start by telling you why I used to think I do it. It was to make the world fairer. If you don't have much money and can't really make ends meet – that's the majority of us students, let's face it – why not help yourself now and again? The sort of people who buy these things do it with their small change anyway."

"Okay," said Julian. "I follow you so far."

"But that's actually not why I do it. No, there's a bit more to it." Julian listened carefully. "It's really because I *can*. I don't feel the nerves, the guilt pangs. At least, not any more. It's almost as if that wallet would have gone to waste if someone with the right skills hadn't taken it. For me, it's about keeping my senses sharp."

"I think I understand," said Julian. "Now, guess what we're going to do next."

"What?"

"We're going to put the wallet back."

Her eyes widened. "What? Are you nuts? We'll definitely get caught. If she sees us again that shop assistant is going to get suspicious."

"Well, that's a risk you'll just have to take."

"Seriously?" She looked like a schoolgirl who had just been told to do a better job of tidying her room.

"Look, I'll make things easier for you. I'll come with you and help, be your accomplice, in a manner of speaking."

"Accomplice? Ha, you're funny. Okay, it looks like we'll be working as a team then. Hopefully they might think you're my dad or something." Julian glared at her. "I'll talk to the girl and pretend to ask some dumb question about the shoes I bought. All you have to do is lurk behind me and put the wallet back on the shelf. It's pretty obvious where it goes. There's only one small section for men's accessories and there's a great big gap where that wallet was."

"All right," said Julian. "Are you ready?" She nodded. Julian took the wallet and put it in his jeans pocket. It felt natural, as if something like that should belong to him. They both walked into the shop, Sonia first. The shop assistant gave her a small smile, then looked at her quizzically.

"I forgot to ask," said Sonia. "About care and maintenance – do I need to get any special polish or protection spray?" The assistant told her to wait while she got some from the back of the shop. Julian had all the time he needed to put the wallet back in its place. He fished it out of his pocket but hadn't realised how much his hands were sweating. He dropped it and cursed. Sonia stared at him. He bent down quickly to pick it up but knocked his knee against a lower shelf as he stood up. Sonia looked at him angrily. His knee hurt and he spent a second or two rubbing it. She rolled her eyes. He managed at last to put the wallet back on the right shelf, but facing the wrong way. At that instant the shop assistant returned, smiled at Julian, and told Sonia that the polish was complimentary. Julian almost burst out laughing.

"Well, that wasn't too terrible, was it?" said Julian outside the shop. "I'm glad you had the chance to do some good. Or reverse some bad, at least."

Sonia stuck her lower lip out at him. "And what's so great about what you do?"

Julian was momentarily silent. "I'm not sure. Let me think about that."

"I'm hungry," she said. "Can we get something to eat?" Julian was too, and told her that was a great idea.

They started to walk towards the section of the high street that had decent restaurants, past Café Franz (not there, she had specified – "somewhere better") and past a curry house that he ate at on his own, far too often for his waist measurement (he would have to get to know Sonia better before taking her there). They walked right in front of the local Italian restaurant, *La Gazza Ladra*, and Julian pointed at it.

"How about here?" he asked.

"Perfect," she said. "I love pasta. I can eat it all day." Julian looked at her small, thin body and wondered when she had last attempted that. They got a table outside – the weather was getting chillier but it was still just about warm enough for al fresco dining – and Sonia ordered a lasagna with a side order of sautéed potatoes, while Julian chose the seafood linguine. She declined his suggestion to share some green vegetables. "Can we have red wine?" she asked.

"If you don't mind drinking most of the bottle. I usually stick to one glass." Julian didn't want to let himself go in the company of someone like Sonia, and besides, he was rather keen to see what effect alcohol would have on her.

"Trying to get me drunk, are you?" she smiled. Julian protested. "Don't worry, it doesn't take long with the size I am."

"So," said Julian after the food had arrived. "Tell me more about Sonia." She was eating quickly (the lasagna had "loads of pasta with just a bit of meat sauce, the way I like it") and taking large, frequent slurps from her wine glass, which the hovering waiter topped up at every opportunity. "This is what I know so far: she is a student of language and literature; an amateur, though highly skilled thief; and of course, a part time–"

Sonia hadn't quite finished her mouthful of potato. "What gives you the right to be so judgemental? And what's so great about what you do?"

"Yes, you asked me that. Well, this is the way the world works. It's basically driven by money–"

"Tell me about it."

"Yes, right. So believe me, I wasn't being judgmental. The point is, there are people who are depending on me, trusting me with their hard earned savings. My role is to live up to that trust. I make sure that people have enough to retire on, and maybe that some other dreams of theirs can come true too. That's what this business is all about. People are investing their money *with* me, but they are also investing *in* me. Do you understand?" Sonia nodded. "I suppose my job is to make people happy."

"What about that old man?"

"Which old man?" Julian felt silly as soon as he said that.

"The one from this morning. When I was in the shop. He didn't look particularly thrilled to me.

"You can't keep everyone happy. He's a trouble maker, that's all."

"I don't think you can handle trouble. I mean, real trouble, something going really wrong."

"Indeed? And what makes you think that?"

She shrugged. "Just a feeling I get. You're too straight. Too nice."

Julian fell silent, a silence he felt uncomfortable with but nevertheless didn't want to break. Sonia looked relaxed. She was eating and drinking at a slower pace, probably because she was quite full by now. "All right Sonia. Let's hear some more about you.

"There isn't much to tell. Honestly." Julian stared at her. "Well, okay, I suppose I do have some sort of story. Everyone does. So, I live with my mother who is a widow. We're not very well off, as you may have–"

"A widow?" Julian felt as if some great mystery had just been answered, though he wasn't sure what exactly. "Tell me about your father. How did he die?" He bowed his head and slapped it. "Sorry. God, what an idiot. What I meant was I'm very sorry to hear your father died."

"That's okay. Will you let me finish? I was just about to get to that. Anyway, as I was saying, my mother and I struggle a fair bit but we're happy. We actually get along really well. She works as a nurse and usually ends up doing the night shift. So I don't actually see much of her."

"Ok. Please, continue."

"She's glad I managed to get into university. She's quite ambitious for me, you know. The thing is, being so short of cash means I'm always trying to do something else on the side. Just to pay my way through."

"I see. So tell me about your father. What happened?"

"It's a long story. Anyway, he died a very long time ago. It seems as if so much has happened since then. I was twelve at the time. I turn nineteen this year, in case you were wondering."

Julian's estimate had been roughly correct. "What did your dad do? For a living."

"He was an accountant. A really good one, and he worked very hard. Long hours, almost every day, practically every week end too. Just to keep me and my mum well provided for."

"Were you two especially close?"

She nodded. "We were. He would spoil me, buy me nice things now and then." She sighed, swallowed a couple of times and looked down at the table. "They accused him of stealing money. Fraud. After all those hours he worked to impress them and make something of our lives. Bastards."

"Oh God, no. Must've been an awful time for you all."

"They dismissed him from his job but couldn't prove anything. They couldn't get any sort of a case together. He took it badly." Julian raised his eyebrows very slightly. "He got depressed and they put him on medication. It didn't do much good, so they tried some new drugs. Nothing really seemed to work. In the end he – he hanged himself." Julian took her hand, gently, by her fingertips. The waiter, who had been trying very hard not to listen, approached carefully, his head lowered. He gestured at the empty bottle and, with a small nod from Sonia, got the permission he needed to take it away. "So, that's something about me. Hope I didn't bore you, Julian."

"Not at all. Seriously, thank you for sharing something so personal with me." She shrugged and Julian squeezed her fingers. She looked down at her plate and started moving the remnants of pasta and potato around with her knife.

"Hello," said a small voice. "I was going to say I hope I'm not interrupting something, but obviously I am. Sorry, I'll just say hi to you both and get lost." They both looked up. It was Rob. There was a mild aroma of beer about him, but no slurring of the speech or unsteadiness. It had just been the one pint then, Julian concluded.

"Hey Rob. Good to see you. What are you–"

"Oh, hi Rob! How are you?" Sonia was standing up and had put her arm on Rob's shoulder. She seemed more excited than at any other time that day.

"Ah, so it seems like you two know each other," said Julian. His wrists were crossed, one index finger pointing at Sonia, the other at Rob. "How, er – where did you meet?"

"It's quite funny, actually," said Sonia. "I was in that pub" – she pointed across the street to the Railway – "waiting for someone, a friend. Anyway, they had loads of old fashioned looking beers at the bar so I thought I'd try one, just totally on a whim. I only ever drink red wine. So this particular beer was called IPA, Indian… pale amber, something like that, and I thought it tasted really strange, but – interesting, really nice, actually - *different*. A bit fruity in a weird way."

"Yes," said Rob. "It looked like she was getting converted. Reminded me of my first time. So, I told her a bit about real ale and how it's brewed. She's a quick learner. And I bet she remembers everything I told her, right, Sonia?"

She smiled and nodded. "Yeah, most of it. I'm considering making it my regular drink. I reckon I'd look pretty good with a pint glass in my hand, what do you think?" Julian pictured it in his mind and tried not to laugh. "But you know what," continued Sonia, "Rob is such a cool guy. He's an engineer. Isn't that fascinating? Designing and creating machines. Real things, stuff people can actually use."

"Well, yes," said Rob, "if you've ever been in a lift and lived to tell the tale, yeah, I suppose you can thank people like me."

"I think it's great that some guys still have real jobs." Sonia began to stroke Rob's chubby forearm. He looked somewhat embarrassed but didn't move. Sonia looked into the distance, squinted and said "I think it's probably time for me to go now."

Julian looked too, squinting even harder for that tall silhouette coming to reclaim what was his. Maybe it was the wine, but he couldn't see anything and wondered if Sonia could. He put his hand on her upper arm, squeezed it a little and said "Goodbye, Sonia. I enjoyed today." He moved his head forward to kiss her on the mouth. She moved her head towards him, angling it to the left just in time for his kiss to land on her cheek. She smiled, looking up at his eyes then turned round and walked off, her large carrier bag jiggling. Julian turned to Rob. "Sit down. Let's have a chat."

Rob hitched his trousers up and sat on the edge of the chair, a position that clearly signalled to the waiting staff that he wasn't going to order anything. "So you had dinner together? Right. This is something I shouldn't mention to Stephanie, if I ever meet her?"

"Sonia seemed quite keen on you, from what I could see. Anyway, tell me Rob, how's work these days? It's true. You're one of the few people I know who actually has a proper job."

"Julian, my company's in trouble right now. There's talk of redundancies, possibly worse."

"I would have thought manufacturing lift motors was the safest market to be in."

"And it is. Normally. The point is the company deposited money at a bank called ITCB – the International Trade and Commerce Bank."

"Yes," said Julian, "I've heard of them. I think they've got a branch around here."

"They're based in Venezuela. Not a lot of people know that, but what most people do know is that they pay a very high rate of interest. The owner of our firm thought, well, why not? He doesn't do things by halves and ended up sticking our entire operating cash in an account with them."

"Right. And the problem is?"

"The problem is as of this morning they have frozen all deposits. They are in serious trouble."

"Okay. So, I guess your company's stuck for a little while? Until it all gets sorted out."

"A little while? No one knows what state this bank is in. There are rumours going around that we only have enough money to pay salaries for one more month. What happens after that, who knows."

Julian nodded. "Is your job safe?"

"No idea. Absolutely no idea, mate." Rob sounded more worried than he looked. How bad could things be? Julian considered Rob lucky to be single, free of the expenses associated with wives and households. "I'll be heading off, Julian. Don't want to be late into work tomorrow with all this going on." Julian folded his arms behind his head and leaned back in the chair. He sighed, feeling slightly annoyed about the way Sonia had turned her cheek to him.

Chapter 6

Julian was reading a letter from Stephanie, which she had sent to him by first class post from the cookery school in Hampshire. He studied her beautiful handwriting on the single sheet of pale green letter paper:

Julian Dearest,

How are you my sweet? We (Allegra and I) are having a fantastic time here at what is, we discovered, Britain's top cookery school. We're learning loads as well, not just about how to manage a kitchen but all about the financial side too (I thought that would impress you!) Juan is a great instructor and very patient with the slower learners in the class.

Actually I've been running some numbers, just on the back of an envelope for now, and I'm thinking we'll need something like £100 000 start-up capital to get our restaurant idea off the ground. Okay, so I could go to mum and dad and ask them to chip in again, but I'm sort of a little embarrassed. Can you help, Jules? I know business is going well for you at the moment. Do give it some thought. A food lover like you will come to the right decision, I just know it!

Anyway, do look after yourself.

Kisses,
Steph xx

Julian reread it, more for the aesthetic pleasure of the paper and ink than anything else. Well, a hundred thousand shouldn't really be that much of a problem for a man such as himself, should it? He had occasionally wondered if Stephanie had chosen to be with him for his money, but usually dismissed that as mere paranoia on his part. But there was something that bothered him: he had known girls at university a lot like Stephanie who had been happy to be friends with him, but had never really shown any interest in going further. And if he was going to be totally truthful with himself, he had to admit that that resemblance had been a large part of Steph's appeal when he had first met her. Julian shifted forward in his chair. No, the money would be no problem at all.

He thought about Sonia and hoped she was enjoying wearing her new shoes. Would she save them for special occasions? It would probably just be dress down (and those scruffy flat sandals) as usual for daily activities, whiling away time in cafes, consuming caffeine and novel reading. He remembered the day they had spent together, the way she had opened up to him and her curious friendship with Rob. The thought of those two spending time together made him laugh. No doubt after her introduction to real ale she would be taking elementary courses in mechanical engineering. Oh, of course – there had been someone else that day: George McCrum, that elderly pain in the rear. Julian had emailed him and told him to come round for a chat whenever he wanted to. That was probably a mistake, Julian realised.

He put down Stephanie's elegant letter paper and opened his email account. He had intended to spend some time searching the internet for commercial premises for her restaurant-to-be, but thought he'd update his inbox first. The two handsome letters he'd received over the last few days reminded him how much he hated email. The ease with which people could communicate their latest silly thought whilst being almost completely excused from the rules of grammar and style contributed directly to the nation's decline. This was emphasised now by the sea of black bold type under the 'Subject' column. 'Inbox(124)' the screen helpfully informed him.

Julian ignored most of the emails (the spam filter only got rid of the most egregious junk) but honed in on McCrum's answer. He was due to come round some time that day. All right, not a problem – Julian could deal with him. But there was something from Sunil Sharma too. Strange; Julian had given him his email address as a matter of course, but until now Sunil had never used it. Julian opened the email and read what Sunil had written:

Subject: Investment Scheme
From: Dr S Sharma drssharma@bigsmiledental.co.uk
To: Julian Kay

Hi Julian

Hope you and Stephanie are keeping well.

Seems like everything's still going fine with this investment, which is just as well. Can't really say the same for some of the other stuff I've put my money into!

Can we meet for a chat? I need to make a withdrawal, not yet sure how much exactly. How about you tell me what my options are when we meet.

When would suit?

Cheers,
Sunil

Ah, a withdrawal. It had to happen at some point. Ultimately every investor would need to take something out, even the high earning, frugal ones like Sunil. Julian supposed that his withdrawal would be a fairly minor one. He sensed what was going on: one of Sunil's other schemes hadn't quite worked out as planned and he was a little out of pocket. So a little dip into something that was working would sort that out. Nothing to worry about – Sunil was a man of means. Julian emailed him back to tell him that meeting up that evening would be fine and he should come over straight after seeing his last patient at the dental clinic.

Withdrawals in general were always a tricky issue in Julian's business. There was always going to be a problem if there were just a few too many, especially if they all occurred at around the same time. And what if they were large withdrawals? Maybe even most of the account? That just did not bear thinking about. It had not happened to him yet, and besides, Julian knew he had the power of financial persuasion on his side, the ever heeded opinion of the trusted investment advisor: "It's best to stay invested. Why spend profits? Long term wealth creation is all about letting your money compound, letting it work for you." The words were his motto and mantra. Julian in fact had only two clients he could truthfully call "takers", that is, regular withdrawers. There was Marek, of course, who needed to pull out the odd couple of hundred here and there for new clothes, a holiday with Maria or a major drinking session with the Polish lads. And Miles, whose withdrawals were much bigger because he had an expensive lifestyle and a vulgar supercar to maintain. But then again, he had deposited a massive chunk of his father's money. The other category was vastly preferable – the "givers". Regular monies deposited, none taken out.

Julian knew most of his clients to date had been sleepers. After the initial deposit they hadn't touched the account. That was his favourite type of investor: trouble free, almost as if they'd done him the favour of dying immediately after giving him their money. The problem was, finding good investors was never easy. It required a considerable degree of studied nonchalance:

appearing in public where the wealthy socialise, making yourself visible (but not obvious), your reputation known (talkative clients were always an asset); yet never seeming keen for new business, making it clear – only when asked, of course – that this was for sophisticated investors only, the select few. There was a degree of artistry to this business and Julian was long past his apprenticeship. But somehow, just recently, it had started to tire him.

He decided to go out onto the streets and find out first-hand what was happening in the commercial real estate market. He wasn't in the mood to speak to agents and anyway Stephanie herself might be better at that sort of thing. They always seemed to enjoy talking to her. At the lower end of the winding high street, the new and recently developed part, coffee shops, estate agencies, tapas bars and a travel bookshop formed a modern north London mercantile community. In a continuous thigh killing near run, Julian powered his way up from his front door to this commercial hub. How busy were the shops? Could you estimate takings by watching the customers, studying how they were dressed, trying to guess how rich they were? Panting, he stood in the middle of the pavement and looked around him. Everyone appeared busy, going about his or her business with a look of grim purpose. Food (particularly of the innovative kind) seemed like the last thing they'd spend their money on, beyond the absolute minimum. Would Julian's hundred grand backing in Stephanie's culinary experiment pay off? Financially, perhaps not, but he knew what the real investment was.

He had last been here three months ago. Something had changed since – but what exactly? Were the restaurant tables emptier, the coffee shops making fewer lattes? He couldn't be sure. There was a closed down shop with whitewashed windows and a large blue estate agent's placard. What had it been originally? Ah yes, an upmarket sandwich bar. Luckily there were three more nearby to service the local workers' lunchtime hunger pangs. Maybe they had cut their prices recently.

Julian thought about what he had seen but saw no need for worry. A restaurant closing down could only mean one thing: the market was over served. That's the problem with any kind of business: someone has a good idea and everybody else wants to copy it. Stephanie was original. Low 'carb' (what an excuse for a word!) Indian food had not been done before and he would be her first regular diner. For the first time that week he missed her deeply.

Julian decided to pop into Café Franz. He couldn't possibly have managed a curry at this time but did rather fancy baked beans on toast. They also did a nice line in young ladies reading novels. He sat down on the too soft, too deep sofa and inhaled the familiar stale air. Even this place felt different. It was half empty, customers were nursing a tea or coffee rather than eating, and some, rather rudely, were just reading newspapers. Julian asked for a large mug of black tea with his beans on toast.

He decided to stroll home. He was tired after his uphill dash. It was late afternoon and Sunil would be round at his house in a couple of hours. Julian didn't mind talking to him, even if this meeting had been a bit sudden. There was something reassuring about his friendly, business-like manner, an aura of having everything under control – which is probably useful if you are a dentist. Even though the walk home was all downhill, Julian felt waves of exhaustion ripple through him. Hadn't he felt this way only few days ago? Was it just the natural aging process? Julian believed he looked much younger than his years would suggest and that it was really all about mental attitude: just act the age you feel. It's only ever oneself that needs convincing. The world believes what you do.

The last few steps to his house were laboured. He yawned, looking forward to an hour's nap before facing Sunil. As he walked towards his front door he saw George McCrum. He had been waiting for him. The old man stood straighter and taller than Julian had ever seen him before, taking a stance with his hands on his hips. "Julian," he said, "I'm glad I caught you. There were a handful of unanswered questions from a few days ago. Just before you sent me on my way, if you remember?" Julian stood still, staring at McCrum and feeling defeated. "The thing is Julian, I'm not really sure what's going on these days. In the economy, in markets all over the world. It's just not going so well. You must have noticed." Julian said nothing, but nodded wearily and thought 'if you say so'. McCrum cleared his throat and looked from side to side. "Look, Julian, don't think I'm not grateful. We've had a very good run so far and I think the profits we've – you've generated in my account have been fantastic. But..."

"Yes?"

McCrum sighed. "I think it's time to call it a day."

"Pardon?"

"I want to close my account and redeem my funds. Look, sorry if I've caught you at a bad time. There's no particular rush, but I'd appreciate a cheque for the full amount in the next few days."

Julian just stared open mouthed for a second or two. He composed himself. "Yes. Okay, that won't be a problem at all. You want a cheque, right?"

"Please. By my reckoning you owe me something like a hundred and eighty thousand pounds. That's the original amount I gave you plus about sixty thousand in interest."

"That sounds about right. I'll look at the paperwork and sort everything out for you." Julian spoke in a monotone. His vision was dimming, his hands and feet feeling numb.

"Well, that's that then, I suppose," said McCrum. "You can just pop the cheque in my letterbox. Anytime." He raised his hand stiffly, as if he had originally intended to shake Julian's, but then thought a goodbye wave would be more appropriate. "And thank you. Thanks, Julian, for all you've done." Julian nodded and McCrum walked home briskly, confidently. All right. Despite the tiredness, Julian's most basic arithmetical mental functions were working. He was about two hundred and eighty thousand pounds down, a sum made up of McCrum's account and Stephanie's start-up capital. That would require some spreadsheet updates. He'd do that after Sunil's visit. He went into the house, sat down in the living room and closed his eyes.

When he opened them again, someone was ringing the doorbell. It rang again, repeatedly. Ah yes, Sunil. Julian got up from a sitting position, felt slightly dizzy and swallowed a couple of times. He opened the door to his smiling, unshaven dentist, briefcase in one hand, a copy of the *Evening Standard* in the other. He looked weary. "Hello Sunil. How was the journey up here?"

Sunil exhaled wearily and rolled his eyes. "Terrible. The tube was totally packed, all the way up from Clapham Common. First hot day of the year, too."

"Do you go down to the south London clinic every day?"

"Twice a week. Still trying to get it off the ground, to be honest."

"I would've thought you'd be taking things a little easier nowadays," said Julian. He led him into the living room. "Sit down. Please."

"Easier? If only. Can't do anything like that, I'm afraid." Julian nodded. "Patients were rather thin on the ground, so we had to cut prices a fair bit. Which means nowadays I have a full schedule, but I'm not really making any profit."

"Oh no."

"I invested quite heavily in the cosmetic dentistry part of the practice. You know, teeth whitening and straightening."

115

"Oh yes, you tried to talk me into having that done. I'm still thinking about it."

"Ha, yes. Well, the point is, I actually borrowed money to expand, and you might say I got a little carried away. I thought demand for this sort of thing was a lot stronger than it turned out to be."

"I see."

Sunil opened his briefcase, pulled out some pieces of paper with scribbles on them and appeared to be studying them. "Julian, the point is, I'm having cash flow problems. Never really thought I'd be saying that, but, yeah, I actually borrowed quite a bit. Far more than I should have."

"I'm surprised. That's not like you, Sunil."

"Yeah, well. What can I say? I've got salaries to pay too. That's my main worry."

"Okay," said Julian, "I did read your email. You need to make a withdrawal, right? How much were you thinking?"

Sunil looked uncomfortable. "Well, a large part of it, actually. If that's possible, of course."

"It certainly is. Instant access at all times, remember? That was in the terms."

"Yes, and I must say you have done fantastically well. I'm really sorry to be having to do this." Julian held his breath and slowed down his heart rate. What would the figure be? How much did Sunil want from him? "Look, Julian, let's do this. I'll keep the original deposit, the hundred grand, invested. But I do need to take out the profits that've been made. Is that okay?"

Sunil had been one of the earliest investors in his scheme. The profits he thought had been generated were in the region of two hundred thousand pounds. Julian clenched his teeth. "Right. Of course, you could withdraw the profits, but think about the compounding. It'd be a shame to stop now, don't you reckon? Alternatively, keep half the profits reinvested. How about that?"

Sunil shook his head slowly. "The most I can keep in there is my original deposit. And that's a stretch. My priority right now is just to clear the debt I've taken on."

Julian nodded. "All right Sunil, leave it with me. I'll check the exact amount of profit you've made and wire you the cash. Is that okay?"

"Yes please, that would be great. Thanks, Julian." He put his hand on Julian's shoulder and left it there for a second. He put his papers back in the briefcase and got up to leave. Julian merely listened for the sound of the front door closing.

How had this happened? Two huge withdrawals in one day? Julian tried to console himself with the realities of the business he was in. A day like today was unusual in any circumstances, something the scheme could handle because of its rarity. Plus, there were new investors on the horizon. He had been working the clubs, his contacts. His reputation was known and there were starting cheques waiting to be signed. Which reminded him: Stephanie's father still owed him money. His name had been in blue type on the spreadsheet for weeks now, pending his starting deposit. Feeling newly energised,

Julian grabbed his car keys from the coffee table and stood up. It was time to drop in on Clive.

He hadn't driven his car for about a week and had a feeling it wouldn't start. It was about ten years old and French. Yes, that's right, a Renault. That was all Julian knew about it, and of course the fact that it often didn't feel like going anywhere. He inserted the key and tried the engine. The starting motor whirred and scraped, painfully, then more slowly, but yes, ignition had taken place and the engine roared, the uncertain weak roar of an aging family car. He drove to the Huntleys' house on the other side of the large, wooded north London hill – fifteen minutes on a weekday evening – and rang the doorbell. A single, measured ding-dong befitting any gas meter reader or Jehova's Witness.

"Hello Julian." Kathleen answered the door, smiling. "I thought that car sounded familiar. What brings you here tonight?"

"Kath, is Clive in?"

"I'm afraid not. Why don't you come in?" Julian shuffled into the spacious living room and sat down on the edge of the sofa. "Would you like a cup of tea? By the way, did you hear from Stephanie?"

"Yes, she's having a great time at her cookery school. Just a glass of water would be perfect, thanks." Kath went to the kitchen and returned with a tumbler filled with slightly sparkling water. "Did Clive say anything to you about my investment fund? Anything about the deposit he was going to make?"

"Clive… yes, he was saying something about that. I think he said something along the lines of not being sure about what you're doing."

"Right. Did he say anything more?"

"He'll be home in a couple of hours. Why not speak to him then, if you don't mind waiting?"

"Actually I can't. Too much work to catch up with tonight. It's just that he was going to have a cheque ready for me. That's what he told me. Do you know if he had a chance to do that?"

Kathleen looked to the side, then at the floor. "He said that he wasn't going to invest because he doesn't like get rich quick schemes. Sorry. Look, perhaps it's just a communication failure. Maybe you could spend more time explaining it next time you meet?" She smiled warmly at him. "You know Julian, I would invest in you. Wouldn't think twice. Trouble is, I've never managed to have very much of my own money."

"Thank you, Kath." Julian got up to leave. His throat felt tight. "Thanks for the vote of confidence." On the way home Julian took every chance he could to thrash his old car, practically flooring the spindly accelerator pedal each time he saw an empty hundred yard stretch of road. The engine protested meekly, but did the best it could. This old heap of gaskets didn't have much time left. This could be the last journey it ever made. Why not?

Why did clients have to be so awkward? Julian tried to cheer himself up by imagining the perfect investor. Very rich, very trusting. Doesn't ask difficult questions, or any questions at all, except maybe "what's the maximum amount I can invest?" No living relatives, and, of course, a heart condition that causes instant death shortly after handing over a big cheque. Julian laughed out loud, in a way that sounded slightly odd to him: panicky, hysterical. Still, one could only hope and wait for that perfect client. They existed. He was sure.

It was still quite early in the evening. Julian thought of Westway House, the source of so many of his most eager investors. The first few guests would be trickling in roughly about now, ordering their initial round of cocktails and maybe a few small plates of the club's signature bar snacks. The dancing would come later, but now... yes, they'd be in the mood to talk, their minds receptive after that first hit of vodka. Julian knew he had a pretty good shot at knocking some funds out of them tonight. Thrashing that poor old engine one last time, he drove down to the club in record time. He found a suitable side street far enough away from it, parked the car at some awkward, barely legal angle and ran straight to the main entrance. Harry seemed to know something was the matter – why the big rush tonight, his eyes were asking – but behaved no differently: "Good evening, sir. It's a pleasure to see you again." Julian nodded his greeting to Harry and rushed past him. He double stepped the flights of stairs up to the bar and dance floor level and flopped down onto the nearest barstool. Gripping the edge of the wood and marble surface with both hands, he took several slow, deep breaths. He needed to be on top form.

So, whom did he have for company tonight? He looked around, without making it too obvious. Sitting a couple of seats down from him was a casually dressed couple, both the man and woman in their thirties. They had ordered a bottle of good red wine (a rioja, from what Julian could see of it) and each had a small glassful held elegantly by the stem. They weren't saying much to each other, indulging only in the occasional small smile or light touch. Somehow they seemed perfectly synchronised, completely at peace with each other. No, that wouldn't work. Not the right sort of people. Julian was adept at detecting dissatisfaction – *tension* – that gnawing sense that despite all the blessings life had conferred, something else (usually more money) was required. Pair that with a sense of entitlement, a feeling that some special opportunity exists for a chosen few (a group into which Julian could grant entry) and you have a customer in the making. All that's needed after that is for the smartly dressed, well-spoken financial advisor to assure the client-to-be that yes, it is perfectly possible to earn thirty percent per year on your money and that's actually what the very rich are doing whilst keeping very quiet about it. A hasty fumble for a pen and the dotted line gets signed.

All right, who else was here? Julian wasn't used to the place being so quiet, or the feeling of urgency, that sense that new investors were actually *needed*. He had always maintained a flawlessly cool demeanour, making them practically beg for a chance to be let in. How times can change. Okay, come on, there must be something in the way of prospects here tonight? He swivelled backwards on the stool and squinted at the entrance. Any newcomers?

121

An older man – portly and well into his sixties – had just entered and was walking slowly towards the bar. Julian knew him. His name was Bill, and tonight he was resplendent in a mauve shirt and large waisted pale blue jeans. He was one of the club's most committed regulars, making an appearance almost every night. Affable and soft voiced, he enjoyed spending hours sitting quietly at the bar with a glass of brandy and soda. Unlike Miles he never made any effort to chase any of the club's female clientele. The unexpected consequence of this was that young women seemed to take any opportunity they could to walk right up to Bill to say hello, start a conversation and give him a friendly hug. If Julian had joined Westway House to meet women rather than customers (oh, to be able to put pleasure before duty!) he would have studied his approach – or rather, that essential lack of approaching – in detail. Although he had noticed that Bill, curiously, paid very little attention to his female admirers, despite being single and highly eligible, preferring instead to have rather intense conversations with the young barman who worked the early shift on week nights. They were, to all appearances, on very familiar terms.

Bill sat down carefully and acknowledged Julian with friendly a raising of the eyebrows. Julian knew he could relax and enjoy a few minutes of stress free chat. Bill was rich already and didn't care to get any richer – certainly not if it meant exerting his intellect by trying to understand something unfamiliar. He was that deadest of dead end prospects: a truly contented man. At least financially.

"Anything new with you, Bill?" asked Julian. It was a rhetorical question. Bill seemed to be the only constant in this late night world of loud music, louder suits, strong cocktails and young(ish) people. "I've got to say, this place seems totally dead. I know it's early still, but – come on!" Julian looked exaggeratedly from side to side, peering at the faces of drinkers and revellers in some totally imaginary crowd.

Bill laughed. "It's been like this for a while. These days it doesn't seem to get going until much later. It used to be ten people ordering two cocktails each at nine thirty. Now? Five people showing up at eleven and nursing a drink till closing time. Everyone's tightening their belts."

Julian couldn't resist a quick glance at his waist. "You reckon?"

Bill nodded. "Something's different. Just these last few weeks. Still, it gives Stefan" – he smiled at the barman – "much more time to talk to me." Julian had a feeling Bill would be tipping generously for his cognac tonight.

He didn't want to interrupt a man in deep congress with his brandy pourer. Nevertheless, Julian was glad to be sitting near them. He wasn't too exposed, too obviously alone. Any curious stares and he could slip seamlessly into their conversation. Yes, he was perfectly positioned. And finally the place *was* starting to fill up. Julian waited for a pause in the conversation, caught Stefan's eye (was that a wink?) and ordered a sparkling mineral water. There was work to be done.

Julian held his breath and listened. Yes, there was a couple of stray voices in the distance, one male, the other female. There was some mild discord in the few traces of conversation he could make out, and the hairs on the back of his neck and forearms bristled at this disturbance in the ether, a perturbation that usually signalled the approach of a potential new client. He looked round. The man and woman were approaching the bar. They sat down near him, politely leaving one stool free as a separator.

"What do you fancy, then?" the man said to his female companion. His voice was matter of fact. It was impossible to gauge his origins by his accent, which was bordering on the mockney whilst still keeping one foot safely in the home counties. He was wearing a pinstripe suit (law, banking?), an oversized Swiss sports watch (a status indicator: this man had acquired some money) and, somewhat incongruously, a brightly coloured woven bracelet. A desire to escape?

His partner was a very thin woman of roughly the same number of years – Julian was good at assessing ages, and judged the three of them to be at the same stage of life – with tightly scraped back hair and a lot of silver jewellery. Her closely fitting pantsuit had clearly been inspired by the hairdo. She was reading the bar menu carefully, her pointed finger with its glossy black nail moving smoothly over its surface. "I want this one," she said. Julian knew the menu well and could tell, by the general area in which her finger was hovering, that she had asked for one of the priciest wines they offered.

Immediately his gaze flipped to the man's face, just in time to see it fall.

"What do you think of wine list here?" Julian said to the man. "I've been a member here for ages but haven't worked my way through it yet."

The man snorted but quickly turned it into a chuckle. "I'm more of a spirits man myself, but yeah, this does look pretty good from what I can tell. Of course, this one here" – he pointed at the woman with his thumb – "she only wants the best."

Julian saw the woman smiling at him. "Well, why not?" he said, "you only live once."

"Ha ha, yes." The man had his wallet out and was trying to decide which one of approximately ten different credit cards to use.

"And," Julian continued, "we all know living costs way too much. Especially in London." They both nodded. "What line of work are you in?"

"Me? Nothing much. Property. I buy houses, do 'em up and sell them on."

"How interesting."

"And I help him," volunteered the woman, "on the design and creative side."

"Ah, so you're the one with the artist's eye!" She laughed and looked away. Julian addressed them both. "So how's the market these days? Roaring, no doubt?"

The man hesitated. "Fine. Really strong. This last month things have softened, but generally it's been all go." The woman agreed enthusiastically. "Right now we've never had so much on the market at the same time," he continued. "We've got a lot invested."

"I see." Julian was leaning towards them.

"So what do you do, then?"

"I'm in the financial markets. Investment management. Foreign exchange, mainly."

"Sounds impressive. I've heard of fortunes being made in that line of work."

"Well, you know." Julian shrugged. "It's been pretty good to me so far. The trouble I'm having – "

"What?" they both said in perfect unison.

"The hardest part is having to let people down. Prospective customers. So many investors want to buy in at the moment that I've had to raise the minimum deposit."

They were staring at him, nodding slowly. "So… it's pretty difficult to become one of your customers?" said the woman.

"I just realised," said the man, "you're sitting there without a drink. Please, have some of this. Barman – one more glass, if you don't mind!"

"Well–" Julian was rather tempted by the expensive vintage.

"No, please, I insist." He filled the small wineglass almost to the top, sloshing some of the dark red liquid, and handed it to Julian. "So, you were saying?"

"Everyone wants high returns with low risk. No surprises there. So far we've managed to produce positive returns each and every month. Touch wood." Julian placed his fist on top of the bar.

"Right," said the man. "So annually, what sort of return are we talking about?"

"So far it's been in the twenty-five to thirty percent range."

The man took a deep breath, appeared to compose himself and said calmly "And what's your minimum investment?"

Julian took one last good look at them. He did a quick calculation in his head based on their age, self-image and lifestyle to arrive at a figure. "Forty thousand pounds." A few more couples like this and his finances would be back to normal.

"Well, that should be no problem for us, should it, Mark?" The woman was looking excitedly at her companion.

"No, none at all. But listen, uh – sorry, I didn't catch your name?"

"Julian Kay." He held out his hand.

"Pleasure, Julian. I'm Mark, this is my partner Lorraine. Listen, we'd love to be invested with you, seriously, but regarding the money – the actual cash transfer, I mean – can you wait for that? A few months, if possible?" Julian frowned at them. "It's just that... *liquidity* is a bit of a problem at the moment."

"I'm sorry?"

"Look, I can assure you, we are solvent. Very much in the black," said Mark. Lorraine nodded forcefully to confirm. "It's just that we're waiting on a few deals to complete. That's all."

Lorraine appeared to have just remembered something. She looked at Mark and scowled. "Mark, was that new beemer really necessary? I mean, we were doing fine with the cash flow. Then you had to go and blow–"

"I don't think that new designer kitchen you insisted on helped much."

"That car costs us more than most people earn."

Mark sighed. "Julian, seriously, can you wait for a while? It won't be long." He had a pleading look on his face.

"No problem." Julian put the half empty wine glass on the bar. He got up quickly and, in one smooth movement, pulled out a business card from his inside pocket and handed it to them. He looked them in the eye and smiled broadly. "Call me as soon as you have the funds available." He didn't expect to be hearing from Mark and Lorraine any time soon.

Before leaving the club, Julian had a quick look around for Miles (he needed a little light relief) but there was no sign of him tonight. He descended the stairs to street level and blankly raised a hand to Harry. The journey home was slow and quiet, a whining, laboured meander back up to north London. The engine didn't deserve to be thrashed again.

Arriving back at his house, he immediately wanted a drink. Being so disciplined, he had not had a sip of whiskey in what felt like months. He looked at the slim square bottle on the kitchen worktop. Two thirds full, just as he had left it. He unscrewed the cap, raised the bottle's mouth up to his nose and inhaled. Delicious. He took a small swig, and then a larger one. The roof of his mouth and throat burned; the vanilla and caramelised sugar overwhelmed him, then died away. He took the bottle and sat down in the living room, thinking he could fall asleep for the night there and then. How rapidly his personal habits were deteriorating. Stephanie had only been gone a few days.

Whiskey was a real man's drink. Julian looked at the bottle in his hand and felt invigorated, powerful. He pictured someone older than him, middle aged, grey but handsome. Tall, sharp features. Very accomplished, undoubtedly wealthy. That's what Julian would become. It was as if he were right there, sitting next to Julian, telling him how much he admired him; that things always got better for the smart and motivated. The people with vision. *Richard Stein.* Thank God for the ideal client, and for the fact he was here with Julian in this time of need.

It was the most effective alarm he had ever been woken by. Pneumatic drills usually did the job better than anything else, but this was as if a tractor and a London bus had taken cocaine and decided to sing a duet. The ground rumbled. The windows buzzed in their frames. Julian opened his eyes and realised it was actually a car of some sort. He was lying at an odd angle on the sofa. His neck ached horribly. He blinked hard several times to get rid of the feeling of his eyeballs being scratched.

The noise stopped. "Julian. I say, Julian!" It was a man's voice, well-bred and impatient. "Julian?" He started banging on the door. "Julian, I want to talk to you!"

Julian walked slowly to the front door, making sure each footfall was gentle enough not to produce another throb in his head. "What is it?" he whispered.

"Julian. Glad I caught you." It was Miles. Possibly the worst sight to wake up to when you are seriously hung over. He was wearing one of his checked suits, the jacket slung over one shoulder. His shirt was partially hanging out, somewhat like his stomach. "We need to talk."

"You talk. I've lost my voice."

"Right." Miles looked him up and down as if to say 'I thought I drank a lot!' and pulled out his wallet. He didn't open the wallet but brandished it, pointing it at Julian. "I need to take some money out of my account. I've come up a little short." Julian jabbed his thumb in the direction of the living room and Miles entered the house, following Julian to the sofa on which he had been sleeping. Miles looked at the wrinkles on it and pulled a face. They both sat down.

"Okay Miles. Good morning, by the way." Miles nodded. "So, you need to make a withdrawal. What – er, how much?"

"Well, quite a lot actually. Things are a little tough at the moment."

"Why's that?"

"Dad. He's decided that he no longer wants to keep paying me my allowance."

Julian, rather irrationally he realised, felt glad that Miles was in a tight spot. It was going to cost Julian money, but he thought he'd enjoy it. Someone like Miles could squirm a bit. It was worth the fun. "Oh dear. Miles,

I'm really sorry about that. Why did he suddenly take this decision?"

"Well he did something stupid. I'm really quite furious with him." He slapped the wallet rapidly against his palm.

"What was that?"

"You must have heard about that bank that went bust recently, right? That South American one. I forget the name."

"Yes, of course. I do read the financial press."

"Right, well. My father had put quite a bit of his cash in an account there. And, well… at this point we have no idea how much we're – he's going to get back. He's not a happy man."

Julian nodded. "Ah. Yes, I see the problem. I have a friend who had money there, too."

"And so he said to me, Miles, this is where it ends. I've been looking after you, supporting you financially your whole life. Now things are a bit tougher for me. I'll survive, he said, but I think you should be more independent. And you know what he did then? He wished me luck. Wished me luck! Can you believe it?"

Julian looked concerned. He felt a little for Miles now. Luck was staying indoors rather a lot these days. "That is tough. Sorry, to hear all this, Miles."

"So, look. I need to start by asking you one thing. How much do I have at the moment? In my investment account?" Julian usually had to look up account balances for the sleepers. He had practically forgotten who they were or what they looked like, but Miles was at the opposite extreme. At the rate he spent money, each and

131

every month required a healthy wad of cash to be withdrawn from the account. The Sunils and McCrums, the frugal and wise, had been financing all of Miles' spending. Until today, of course.

"You have about a hundred and eighty-seven thousand in your account. Give or take a few hundred quid."

"What?" said Miles, looking as if a second injustice had just been done to him. "No, that can't be right. I've got a lot more than that."

"No you haven't, Miles. Remember all the withdrawals you've made. I've got a long list of them, all written down." Julian had always had mixed feelings about Miles. As one of the most inveterate 'takers' he was a financial liability. But on the other hand he was a *talker*, someone who spoke of Julian's prowess all over the city's nightclub scene. And that had paid off. His Lamborghini had done an enormous amount of marketing for Julian (though he still couldn't stand the sound of it).

Miles appeared to be thinking, remembering the details of credit card bills, bar tabs, expensive dinners, tanks of petrol and bodywork repairs. "I think you might be right. Hmm."

"Shall I send you a cheque?" Julian's voice was a croak.

Miles let out a huge sigh from his enormous barrel chest. "Yes. That would be the best thing to do." He waved goodbye to Julian with his wallet, put it in his back pocket and walked out towards his car. Julian fixed his eyes on the back of his fat neck and playfully imagined delivering a single, fatal punch. He put his fingers in his ears as Miles started the engine and drove off

Julian usually liked to look at himself in the mirror, particularly for any newly emergent grey hairs. Right now he realised a mirror was superfluous if he looked anything like the way he felt. No, what mattered now was drinking – that is, hydration as opposed to intoxication. He settled on the tea strategy: several cups of Earl Grey and Darjeeling in strict alternation. He made the very first cup, swallowed half of it whilst still very hot and sat down on the sofa with the rest of it.

Perfect investors were a mirage. A fallacy. All they would ever do is let you down. Julian did some quick mental addition and realised his scheme owed several hundred thousand pounds. That was money that was due to be paid in the next few days. He had used a lot of the early investors' deposits to buy this house – or rather, put a large down payment on it. There was still money owing on the mortgage. Julian had always been worried by his own living expenses, and as a result was a careful spender, always making sure Stephanie and her needs came first. Of course, he should have been prepared for a day like this. What an amateur. He would have stood up and kicked himself if he hadn't been in enough pain already. He took a sip of his tea.

Stein probably still had faith in him. He trusted him with his money. How much of his total wealth did that cheque represent? Enough for him to mind if it went missing? *You wouldn't want to let me down.* Yes, he probably would mind. There was one calculation that

Julian found so irresistible that he carried it out in his head again and again, enjoying its arithmetical perfection, thinking about what the numbers meant. Stein's deposit was easily large enough to cover what he owed: Stephanie's start-up costs plus the money he had to return to McCrum, Sunil and Miles. There was even cash left over to pay off the remaining balance on his mortgage and a full year's living expenses on top. How interesting.

Stein and Julian had had an instant bond. It was as if two talented men of business, alone in a world of mediocrity, had suddenly experienced a meeting of minds. How quickly Stein had handed over his cheque. He had already known the calibre of man Julian was. He had recognized himself in him. Beyond that there were no further questions. Without a doubt, Stein met all the criteria of the perfect client – not to say the ideal man; a faithful friend, too. Wealthy, cultured (Julian ran through part of Stein's classical music collection in his mind) and well mannered, prepared to trust without interference. The very embodiment of Julian's ideals. One thing, though. Richard Stein was still very much alive. Living clients had an annoying way of asking for their money back when you least expected it.

Julian knew that every great man at some point had to pass the mantle on, hand over his knowledge and experience. And money. The challenge of succession, that was the ever present burden for a man of status. Stein had achieved so much in his life. What if he were to meet an accidental death? That would rather poetically complete the circle.

Oh yes, there was one more thing. Julian had it on good authority that Stein was not a very nice person. What if his death were not all that accidental?

Chapter 7

I don't think you could handle any real trouble. You're too nice. What had Sonia meant by that? Apart from the literal meaning of the words – it was pretty obvious Julian had never been in a street brawl or gunfight – what had she really been trying to say? That he was weak? Yes, maybe. And perhaps that was why she was spending so much time with Rob. With him you got exactly what you expected: beer, earthy jokes and lift motors. He could probably put up a set of shelves in a couple of hours. Julian had tried once, and didn't intend to again.

On this particular morning, despite having no appointments arranged, Julian had made a special effort to shower, shave and wear clean clothes. The last couple of days had been embarrassing. Even Miles had been shocked to see him. The very idea of having fallen apart so rapidly – after less than a week of Stephanie's absence – scared him. What if she came back to discover he had reverted to a second year engineering student? Would it all be over? Financially it was looking as if things were headed that way.

But then again, Julian felt, perhaps he shouldn't be so hard on himself. He had been through an awful time. After almost three years of running his investment scheme – helping others always having been his main goal – what had he got to show for it? What had he done for himself? To date he had bought a blue silk dressing gown, that Savile Row suit, a box of ten large Cohiba cigars and a fancy gas flame lighter. He became aware of an overwhelming new emotion rising up in him, something he felt was coming right up to his throat. Julian normally didn't get distracted by emotions, but this one was curious. He wanted to have *fun*. Splash out, not so much financially (although he knew cash would probably be required) but spiritually. The thrill of jumping off the side of a yacht (shouldn't he have been able to afford one by now?), downing a bottle of champagne with most of it running down your chin, kissing a girl hard then pushing her away (ideally over the side of that yacht.) What had happened? His career had been one of hiding, creeping, being the one who never stood out. It was time to be himself. Or rather, a more daring version of himself.

Julian picked up his smartphone and typed out a text message to Sonia: "Hi, how's it going with Dostoyevsky? Managed to finish it yet?" He realised that had been a somewhat strange message for someone whose mind was set on having fun.

"Just finished reading it. Have to write a *very* long essay now. Crap! :)"

"Ok. Good luck with it. When do you think you'll be finished?"

"Depends. What did you have in mind?"

Julian weighed up various possibilities. What would a nineteen year old girl consider fun? Something that a man twice her age might know about? They had already been shopping; he had to think of something else to tempt her. He typed back: "Sonia, have you ever been to a casino?"

"Oh wow yes but that was ages ago. Def'ly want to go again! X" Julian smiled slyly. He had known she would like that. No doubt she had discovered a new way to cheat the house; probably something as simple as swiping a couple of high value chips when the croupier is distracted. He resolved to keep a close eye on her.

"Ok. Meet me at 9. Same place?"

"The café? Yes, cool, I can't wait! XX"

Julian had ordered a taxi. As it drove uphill to their meeting point, he wondered if she would be wearing the shoes he had bought her. The cab pulled up to where she was waiting. He saw that she was on her own and inferred that some unspoken agreement had been struck between her outsized minder and himself. Julian opened the door, taking a good look at her outfit. Yes, she was wearing the shoes. That, at least, was a good sign. He shifted his gaze upwards. A pair of black leather leggings (not too shiny) and a long, loose silk top, the same dark red as the shoes but with a design. Was her hair longer, too? Julian was impressed. Sonia looked like a young... woman, he had to concede.

"Hi!" she said sweetly. "I'll just squeeze in here." She sat next to him and he moved up. "You know I can't really remember the last time I went to a casino. It's so exciting. You never know what's going to happen."

"You generally just lose all your money. That's what happens." Sonia pouted and nudged him. "But then, what would I know? I'm not a gambling man."

"Oh come on Julian. I don't believe that for one minute."

"How far did you get with that Dostoyevsky essay?"

"About five hundred words." She bit her lower lip, which Julian had by now worked out was her guilty look.

"Well, it's a start."

"You could say that. My mother thinks I'm a slacker."

"You know what, Sonia? I used to write. Books, I mean. Novels. I got a bit further than five hundred words, but never actually finished one."

"Do you still write?" She sat up straighter.

"No time, these days. Just far, far too busy." Julian wondered what all the desperate activity over the last three years had really been for.

"That's a shame. Were you any good?"

"You know Sonia, I think I could have become pretty good. I have a good imagination."

"Oh, definitely. You've got one hell of an imagination." She looked as if she were suppressing a laugh. The suppression failed and a torrent of giggles poured out.

"What's so funny? Anyway, I'm glad to see you so happy. Makes a change from last time."

She nudged him again. "Just excited, that's all. By the way, where are we going, exactly?"

"West London. It's a pretty smart place. You'll like it." Westway House had a casino on the floor immediately below the bar and disco. Customers usually started off there, then walked up a flight of steps to drink away their losses. There had been some huge losses recently if the bar bills were anything to go by.

"Thank you," she said, and squeezed his hand.

The cab stopped outside Westway House's main entrance. "Good evening," said Harry. "It's a pleasure to see you again, sir." He looked at Sonia and raised his straightened hand to his head as if saluting. "Good evening, ma'am. I wish you a very pleasant evening." Sonia beamed at him. "And the very best of luck, too, if you'll be trying your hand at the tables."

"He seems to know you quite well. Seems like a nice guy," Sonia said to Julian.

"Harry? Yes, he's a been a great help to me."

They pushed past the crowd at the door and walked up two flights of stairs, straight to the casino floor. Julian wasn't familiar with this part of the club and looked around at the dark red interior. It was a very close match for Sonia's shoes and top. She stood still and stared at the roulette table, fascinated.

"Ah, roulette," said Julian. "Don't bother. You'll never win at that. The odds are fixed against you." She looked at him a little witheringly. "But, look, there's no harm trying. Let's see how you get on with this, to start off with." He handed her a hundred pounds in twenty pound notes. She took it and dashed to the cashier's counter, then walked straight over to the roulette table. She stood at the side and watched for a while. Julian joined her, standing at her side, and saw she was holding five chips.

He looked at her. She stared at the slowly spinning wheel and whizzing ball. Many spins later, after tens of thousands of pounds worth of chips had been placed, won, lost, mourned and clamoured for, after the croupier's calls for "no more *bets* please" had sent him hoarse, she was still observing. Not just the table, but the facial expressions and behaviour of the other gamblers.

"Well?" Julian said.

"Okay," she said, "Now." She put one of her five chips on the number nineteen. The wheel span, the ball whizzed and she lost her bet. Julian frowned at her. Betting on single numbers was foolhardy. Her face remained blank. Again, she placed a chip on the number nineteen. The ball whizzed, lost momentum and bounced capriciously around the wheel before settling on number twenty-one. Close, but not good enough.

"Sonia, that's a risky way of betting. Why not try red or black?" She swivelled her eyes towards him very briefly and focused on the table again. She took another chip, clenching the two remaining ones in her fist. She put it on that same number, nineteen. The wheel span, the ball slowed down and did its bouncing routine. The wheel was still rotating quite fast by the time it settled on number – Julian held his breath – nineteen… and remained there. "Well done!" he said.

"My lucky night, I suppose." She handed her two unused chips to Julian and collected her winnings: seven hundred pounds (in seven handsome looking white and gold chips) plus her original twenty pound chip.

"Beginners luck?"

"What makes you so sure I'm a beginner?"

"Ok. There's probably some sort of strategy. Number nineteen. That's your age, isn't it?"

"Next time I'll use your age." She pouted cheekily. "But… I don't think the numbers go that high." Julian mouthed 'haha' at her and noticed how different she looked. Her skin shined, her eyes glistened with light from the overhead chandelier. "Can you wait here a moment, Julian? He nodded and she took her chips over to the cashier, exchanging them for a healthy looking wad of twenties. She put most of them in a small pocket located on the inside of the waist of her leggings and walked downstairs with the rest, holding them between finger and thumb. She came back up a couple of minutes later, empty handed.

"Where did you go, Sonia?"

"Downstairs. Just to have a quick chat with Harry."

"Harry?"

"I gave him a hundred. He wished me luck, remember? And it worked."

"Gosh. Well that was pretty generous." Julian knew his own tipping at Westway House had never been particularly lavish. All part of the vital act of remaining low profile. "You're right though," he said. "Once you've got the staff on your side, you're made."

"I know that better than anyone. So, I think you're supposed to buy me a drink now, aren't you?" She looked up at him from under her fringe.

"Absolutely," said Julian, "Let's go upstairs to the main bar." He held her hand, gently by the fingers, and led her up the final flight of stairs to the club's disco. It was still quiet. Small groups of people, who would transform into wild dancefloor gyrators in an hour or two, were sitting around on the armchairs and sofas, staring at the cocktails on the tables in front of them without touching them. Julian found a cosy looking two person leather couch and motioned for Sonia to sit down. He sat next to her. "What would you like to drink?"

"Champagne, please," she said.

"I thought so." Julian looked around for a server, but they were all standing in a little group at the bar. It was a little too early for them to be circulating, catching customers' glances with a friendly smile. The big tipping would start much later. He got up and walked over to the familiar wood and marble bar.

"A bottle of your finest champagne, please." He had never said that before. He wanted to laugh.

The barman had served Julian a couple of times in the past and smiled at him. "Well, sir, we have a bottle of the '85 Bollinger at five hundred and fifty pounds?"

So what? He was going broke anyway. "Two glasses, please," he said, and gave the barman his credit card. He turned round, holding the ice bucket containing the bottle in one hand and the pair of champagne stems in the other. He looked over to where Sonia was sitting. About ten feet from the couch he saw Miles, striding along quite purposefully, headed to the bar. His path was about to cross the space right in front of Sonia. Julian watched. Miles turned round and looked at Sonia, eager, no doubt, to get an eyeful of a pretty young girl. Sonia looked up, and for about half a second they looked straight at each other. They both smiled nervously and quickly looked away, Sonia at the floor. Miles continued towards the bar and Julian set off back towards Sonia, nodding at Miles as they passed. Sonia had been trying to suppress a smirk, but all traces were gone by the time Julian sat down.

"That looks amazing," she said, pointing at the bottle. "Pour me some, quick." Julian tilted one of the champagne stems, filled it slowly almost to the top and handed it to her. He then poured himself half a glass, leaving it on the table. Sonia held her glass just below her mouth and dipped the tip of her tongue into it a couple of times. A look of minor revelation appeared on her face. She took a sip. "Gorgeous," she said. "I reckon we'll get through the first bottle pretty fast."

Julian picked up his glass. "Sonia," he said, "Have you met up with Rob recently?"

She thought for a second and shook her head. "No. Why do you ask?"

"I was just wondering what you two talk about. You're quite a fan of ale, right?"

She looked at her glass of champagne. Its presence seemed to cloud her memory of ever having drunk ale. "Yes, I think I'm developing a taste for it."

"I see," Julian nodded.

"He's just a really nice guy. And very interesting to talk to." Julian frowned. "Hey, don't get jealous. It's nothing more than friendship." She looked up and pointed behind Julian's shoulder. "I think a mate of yours wants to say hello."

Julian turned round. It was Toby, dressed in jeans and a silk shirt, holding a tall, slim glass of lager. There was much less grey in his hair than usual. "Hi Julian. Glad to see you out on the town. You've been hiding yourself away recently."

"Hello, Toby."

"So this must be... Steph–"

"Toby, this is Sonia. Sonia, this is my friend Toby. He's a detective."

"Really?" said Sonia, sitting back and waving at him. He acknowledged the wave with a smile and a nod.

"You know, Julian, I'm really beginning to like this place. Just something about the people you meet here. Thought I'd pop in tonight and find out what's going on."

"Is Heather here too?"

"Actually no. I told her to come over later when she's finished at the shop. Let's see. If she doesn't, looks like I've got a pass for the night."

Julian gestured at the armchair opposite the couch they were sitting on. "You may as well sit down and join us." Toby sat down with his drink. He was just far away enough from Julian and Sonia to have to strain to partake in their conversation. He sat back in the chair, looking around the club but glancing at them every now and then.

"Sonia," said Julian, leaning towards her. "What did you mean when you said you didn't think I could handle trouble? You said that I'm too straight, too nice."

Sonia looked blank. "Did I say that?"

"Yes, that time we went shoe shopping, remember?"

"Oh yes." She thought deeply. "Basically I meant that you've had an easy life. Compared to most people, that is." She had almost finished her third glass of champagne. Julian had given up trying to fill her glass.

"Really? Is that all?" Julian took a quick look at Toby, who seemed to be in world of his own, alternating between gazing at the girls in the club and into space. Julian moved even closer to Sonia. "Tell me, what's the worst thing you've ever done? I think we've got shoplifting as the baseline, but anything worse than that?"

"I killed someone once."

"What?" Julian almost shouted and Toby looked at them. They both smiled reassuringly at him and he went back to his reverie.

"Don't be silly Julian. Of course not. I find it hard to swat an insect. I told you why I swiped stuff. Anyway, I've stopped doing that. For good."

"Do you think I could kill?"

"No!" She looked surprised, then started giggling. The champagne must have had something to do with it.

"But you're doing something pretty bad right now, aren't you?"

"What?"

"Cheating on Stephanie." Thanks for that, Toby.

"But Sonia, listen," Julian cleared his throat and continued. "Killing is sometimes justified, don't you think? In certain, special cases."

"If you're in the army I suppose. A war or something," she said.

"Isn't that just governments getting ordinary people to do their dirty work and die for them?" She looked thoughtful. "The point is, some people are better off dead," Julian stated.

"How can you say that?"

"Well, evil people. Mass murderers, people like that."

"True," she said, "but why would you take it upon yourself to kill them? What

about the police, the government?" Her eyes widened. "What about God?"

Julian wondered if prayer could be an effective financial option. At this point anything was worth a try. "Sonia, suppose someone was threatening your family. Someone evil. And if that person were out of the way, they – the people close to you – would be safe. What about then?"

"Then yes, definitely. Do it." Her answer was instant.

"Hey! You two seem to be having a pretty serious chat!" Toby had leant over and was smiling at both of

148

them. "What's the topic of conversation? Anything that would interest me?"

"No, I doubt it Toby," said Julian. Just an everyday conversation about killing. Nothing that would interest a policeman.

Sonia had stood up. She grabbed hold of Julian's hand and pulled him up. "Come on," she said, "let's dance." She led him to the dance floor. On the way there she cupped her hand and whispered something in his ear. "You know, my ex-boyfriend once killed someone." Julian raised his eyebrows. "Yes, him. The guy you think is my pimp."

She held his shoulders lightly and started rotating her hips rhythmically from side to side. Julian stiffly followed her lead. She moved closer as the music grew louder and the tracks changed from commercial to techno, trance like sounds. The laser beam lights flashed frenetically, flipping from red to green, disorientating him. She danced faster and moved even closer to him. He held both her hands and moved her torso right up to his so they were fully in contact. They gyrated up and down and twirled each other. He looked at the bare skin on her neck and shoulders. Just the faintest sheen. Apart from walking, Julian had not exercised for a while, but sheer excitement fuelled his limbs. He kept up the pace as they danced through ten ever more hypnotic dance tracks. Sonia was sweating by now and her hands seemed too damp to hold. He made a tired face at her. "Okay," she said, pulling his hand, "let's sit down."

Toby, who had been relaxing in the same place with his beer, sat up and smiled when they came back to their couch and sat down. "I saw you dance," he said, "Impressive."

"My feet hurt," said Sonia. She slipped off one of the red stilettos and placed a slender bare foot on Julian's knee. "Any chance of a foot rub?" she smiled.

Julian bent down and kissed the top of her foot, then pushed it away. "I think I'll have to get to know you better first," he said, winking. He leant forward and kissed her on the mouth. She responded enthusiastically, wrapping her arms tightly round his neck. She kissed him harder, more forcefully. With her arms clasping him tightly, Julian stood up. She kept her hold and, as she was pulled up, wrapped her legs around his waist, leaving the discarded shoe on the floor. She looked closely into Julian's eyes so that the tips of their noses were touching. Smiling dreamily, she stuck her tongue out, a second later inserting it into his mouth. She repeated this manoeuvre a few times, reminding Julian of the taste of that expensive bottle of Bollinger. He placed his hands on her buttocks and was surprised at their fullness. He glanced to the side to see what Toby made of all this (he hadn't yet been introduced to Stephanie). Toby hadn't been paying attention. When he saw Julian look at him he smiled and gave him a single thumbs up.

Julian eased Sonia back down onto the sofa. "Please," she said, "can I have some time alone? I'm totally hammered. Give me a few minutes to recover." He remained standing and looked around, enjoying the febrile noise and confusion, the animated mass of bare female backs and arms. Well, this was the fun he had desired – the one week of adult life after years inside the chrysalis – and things were only just getting started. He walked to the bar, determined to do some real drinking. Champagne had its uses, of course, but right now whiskey was required. Julian asked his barman friend for a double of his favourite twelve year old. It disappeared in one sip followed by a large gulp. He nodded and raised his eyebrows, signalling to the barman that another of the same was required. This one slipped down slowly and evenly, warming his gullet rather than burning it. Yes, it's always the second one that achieves that perfect level of measured excitement. He was ready to circulate, socialize, mark out his territory. He ordered one more double – no, make that a *quadruple* – to hold in his hand, walking around liquor to keep him company as he observed, made introductions, chatted and flirted.

Where to start? There was a tall brunette wearing strappy heels and a playsuit standing next to him. She had her back turned to him. He tapped her on the shoulder. "Hey," Julian said, and raised his glass. She smiled politely, took a quick look at Julian's glass and turned round again. Maybe she was a little shy? She probably had a latent desire to dance. He took hold of her hand and pulled. She turned round to face him and mouthed "no thanks." Perhaps her friend – smaller, rounder, sweeter looking – would be more up for it? Julian grabbed her shoulder and started gyrating. She laughed and joined in, but before she could get carried away the tall brunette frowned at her. The smaller one waved a good natured bye-bye to Julian and went back to her companion.

He sauntered over to the dance floor. There was still half of his whiskey left – no immediate need for a top up. He stood at the edge of the expanse of shuffling, swaying, flailing revellers, most of whom were exactly what Julian had once been: office workers with annoying colleagues, too much work and a difficult boss. The price of a steady pay cheque. This was a night of abandon, of unembarrassed wildness, before their weekday duties started once again. His eyes moved from one dancer to the next, boyfriend to girlfriend, colleague to colleague, friend to friend. What were they up for tonight? How far would they go to forget their week? Julian finished off his whiskey and placed the glass on the edge of someone's table. He strode confidently onto the dance floor and made his way right to the centre. He was going to forget all the bad things that had happened to him in the last few days. The music was loud and dancing couples were bumping into him, smiling after a particular hefty buffeting, as if he were an integral part of their enjoyment. There were lovers dancing close up, friends keeping their distance, laughing at each other; men in late middle age wearing suits, convinced they had drunk enough to be excused from any sense of shame. Julian lifted his head to see what was going on in the outer reaches of the floor. In one corner he saw Miles dancing, on his own, and not up to his usual standard. He looked distracted, distant; there was none of the familiar sense of a drunken elephant. He kept to his own space.

A girl – thirties, nice looking – approached Julian, smiled and waved her hand. Julian squinted. His eyes were getting blurry. Ah yes: Heather. They mouthed a 'hi' to each other and started dancing, an arm's length apart, as if Toby's absence was an irrelevance. Where was Toby? Julian wondered but then decided he couldn't be bothered to ask. He had probably gone home after a couple more solitary beers. Julian and Heather circled each other, smiling intermittently, now and then avoiding the other's gaze. Just then a slim fair haired woman, slightly above average height walked rapidly across the dance floor, cutting right through the space between Heather and Julian. He could have sworn it was Stephanie. Yes, he was sure – she looked exactly like her. Was she back early? Who had brought her to this place?

Having reached the optimal state of intoxication, Julian decided it was time to leave. He was sure Stephanie (if that's who it was) hadn't recognised him. Her eyes had been fixed to the floor. He nodded at Heather, raised a hand to say goodbye and went to find Sonia. Sonia – now, where could she have got to? He had left her on the sofa in a pretty tipsy state. There was a chance she was still there, sobering up. Toby would have been keeping an eye on her. Julian retraced his steps back to where they had been sitting. No, neither Toby nor Sonia were there. Right, he'd have to find her. He did a very quick reconnaissance of the whole floor, then went downstairs to the casino. No sign of her anywhere. Okay, she was probably outside talking to Harry (those two had hit it off brilliantly). But no, she wasn't there either. Odd. Julian had one final idea. He walked round to the side of the building, where the smokers and hipsters hung out. Maybe that was her scene? But again, no sign of her. She had probably just made her own way home. Or had arranged for a certain heavily built man to pick her up.

Julian started walking along the main road towards central London. He passed the turning for Miles' house and kept walking. He walked fast, purposefully, eyes fixed on the ground. The temperature was cooler, breezier. The air was perfect for a long, brisk walk, maybe even all the way home.

"Hey you," said a girl's voice. "You're in a state." Julian didn't look up but knew who it was from the dark red high heels. "Are you going to go home looking like that?"

"Well... er..." Julian remembered something about Stephanie returning early from Hampshire. Would she be at home waiting for him? He'd have to text her. "I don't think so. Sonia... can you suggest a better idea?"

Sonia looked impeccable, far taller and shapelier than Julian remembered; definitely an attractive young woman. She had done an unbelievable job of freshening up. Her hair was smooth and shining. She stood very straight in her heels, practically looking Julian in the eye. "Actually I know some people who live around here."

"Really?"

"Yes. And I happen to know of a party going on."

"Where?"

"A few steps from here. I think we should go. I've got a strong feeling it'd be just your kind of thing, Julian."

Julian wanted to make the excuse of being tired (and much older than her) but he felt strangely energetic, refreshed, as if he'd just had his morning tea. "Ok, you lead the way."

She took his hand, very lightly, and pulled him into a small mews side street that he'd walked past several times but never actually entered. It had always seemed too quaint and winding to house anyone living in the modern age. A hundred and fifty years ago the servants and horses would have suffered it. She led him down an iron spiral staircase, alarmingly steep and narrow, that seemed to go on forever. Was it just the stiffness in his legs after all that dancing? He felt no discomfort, just the sense that they were descending several floors below ground level. Not too surprising, Julian thought. Sonia's friends were probably poor students who could afford nothing more than a cramped basement. They finally reached the bottom of the spiral stairs. Julian looked directly upwards, trying to see the sky; surely it should have been light by now? He saw nothing but a coiled mass of spiralling black iron.

Directly in front of them was a forbidding looking dark red front door. Sonia leaned into it and pushed: it opened smoothly. Someone had been expecting them. They had entered a basement flat, laterally very large, but with an uncomfortably low ceiling. Julian could just about stand upright, and even Sonia (in those heels) didn't have much head clearance. The atmosphere was extremely hot and stifling, as if the occupants loved nothing more than turning the heating on full blast in midsummer. They also seemed to have somewhat questionable taste in lighting. Apart from the fact that the main lights were switched off, or dimmed to the point of being practically extinguished, the owner had a large and proudly displayed collection of lava lamps. Oleaginous floating clouds of red, orange and purple cast their cloying glow onto the walls and ceiling. Yes, Julian understood the effect the owner had been trying to create: man living inside a volcano; hot, enclosed, impossible to escape from. His eventual crematorium. What had Julian done to end up here?

"Interesting place," he said to Sonia.

"Yes, I knew you'd like it. Different, isn't it?" Julian nodded slowly. "Why don't you circulate, talk to people? Lots of your friends are here." Julian hadn't recognised anybody. In fact, the place had looked empty when he'd entered. He blinked hard and looked around. Ah yes, he must have been asleep. There were lots of people at this party. All huddled together, talking intensely, feverishly. And they looked very familiar. Where to start? Why not the couple next to him? Julian moved closer to them to listen. Oh right, yes, it was Toby and Heather. Julian was glad they had actually found each other back at the club.

"Toby, those tiles you ordered. Honestly."

"I did my best. It took me hours."

"I really do wonder about your taste. They were unbelievable."

"Hello you two," said Julian, "still on about the decorating work? Yes, I know, I've been there. Both halves of a couple never have the same taste." Either it was the heat in the flat or the distance Julian was standing from them, but they didn't hear him. They didn't even look at him.

"And what about that wallpaper? For a start, wallpaper – these days?"

"I went to that website you told me about."

Julian looked from one to the other and decided not to bother with any further attempts at butting in. He hadn't left the entrance hall so far. He decided to explore the rest of the apartment and find out whom else he might know. He entered the main reception. The same low ceiling, its lack of height emphasised by the much larger floor space. There was quite a crowd in here and the air seemed even warmer. Julian undid two more shirt buttons. He looked at as many of the faces as he could make out in the red light.

Then, all at once, he saw three that he knew well. They belonged to Sunil, McCrum and Miles, all three men having a serious discussion about – well, Julian, most likely. Exactly how... oh well, word of mouth, internet forums and all that. Word gets around. Julian stared, then felt he shouldn't make it obvious and tried to hide behind a tall gentleman standing next to him, who smiled and moved aside slightly to make room for him. Julian paid close attention to their body language. He wished he had learned to lip read. Sunil was explaining something quite complicated to McCrum, who was looking up at him. Miles was half listening, half looking around the room. He was shifting his massive weight from one foot to the other, probably assuming that as this was a gathering of more than ten people, it was only a matter of time before the dancing started.

Julian decided to keep moving. He was sure there were other people he knew here, a good chance of a decent conversation. He slipped out of the reception and back into the corridor. Heather and Toby had gone home. Why not try the kitchen next? At any party the liveliest banter would be happening around the hearth. He walked down to the end of the corridor. Just before the entrance to the kitchen he heard a familiar, friendly voice.

"You young chaps. I really must say, Julian, it does look very impressive. It's all down to you young chaps these days, I've always said that."

"Hello Paul. Nice to see you here," said Julian. At least someone was in the mood to talk to him.

Paul pulled out a large desk calculator from his inside pocket (how had it managed to fit in there?) "I'm an accountant, you know. I've probably already told you that, but yes, I'm usually pretty cautious." He focussed hard on the calculator, bashing out a furious sequence of keys, his brow wrinkled with concentration. "My clients pay me for it. They pay me for it!"

"Right, that's good to know, Paul." Julian moved off into the kitchen. It looked far more promising: much less of that ubiquitous red light in there. He stepped through the doorframe and passed Marek, holding a bucket of paint in one hand and a trowel in the other. When he saw Julian he raised his eyebrows by way of greeting. "Hi Marek, looking busy. It's all go with you!" said Julian. Marek grinned at him, put his bucket and trowel down and mimed drinking from a glass with his hand. He walked over to the kitchen counter and helped himself to a half litre can of lager. "Marek, listen, we'll probably have a lot of work for you and the boys pretty soon. Stephanie's opening a restaurant. It's early days yet, but I think we're going to be starting from scratch, you know, buying a shell and doing it up. Are you on for it?" Marek looked at Julian but kept drinking, in one continuous sequence – as if executed by a workshop machine tool – of mouthful followed by gulp, a five degree increase in the tilt of the can and a reset to the start of the cycle. The lager can appeared to be bottomless, to hold far more than the half litre it was supposed to. Marek's drinking was legendary and this was a chalice worthy of any Slavic hero. Finally sated, Marek raised his thumb to Julian (a gesture of both agreement and jubilation), crushed the laws-of-physics-defying can and dropped it on the floor. It fell under the force of gravity like any regular lager can.

Speaking of drink, there was someone next to Julian who had consumed far too much. He was lying on his back, his legs slightly apart, one knee bent. He had short, plump arms and legs and a large stomach. A lot like... Rob. Oh god no, it was Rob. Julian felt scared. Rob was usually such a good drinker, a man who paced himself, didn't mix his liquor and always chose quality (though never, admittedly, at the expense of quantity). In all Rob's years as a professional level imbiber, Julian had barely heard him slur his words. And now this? Julian realised he was feeling cold, in spite of the infernal heat inside the flat. He looked at Rob's face. It was rocking from side to side, the mouth slightly open. His eyelids were only partially closed, and his eyes had rolled upwards, back into his head. All in all, it was looking bad. How much had he drunk exactly? Julian bent down. He moved closer to Rob's face. Alcohol? No smell of it. None whatsoever. Julian knew that even a single beer can be detected on someone's breath. The rest of the kitchen reeked of supermarket best buy lager, but Rob, oddly, smelt mildly of fabric conditioner and nothing else.

Julian stood up slowly. Should he call someone? There didn't actually seem to be anything wrong with Rob. He was awake, just not especially in the mood to communicate. Or stand up. Nobody was paying him any attention, as if a somewhat overweight man lying on the kitchen floor looking disorientated was entirely normal. Julian was a guest here. He decided it wasn't his role to do anything.

He took one last look around the kitchen before heading off. Anyone interesting, anyone he knew who wasn't in a very weird frame of mind? He thought momentarily of drugs – was that why everyone was so disconnected from him? Julian had tried various illegal substances but had never felt they were of any real use to him. They had never got him into the right circles. No, drugs weren't the issue here; it just wasn't that sort of crowd. But he was determined to find out what was.

He was about to exit the kitchen when he noticed, in the far corner, a man and a woman standing next to each other. Yes, he knew them. Where had he seen them before? He moved nearer to them. They were close enough to be touching and were looking into each other's eyes. Their attire was peculiar, to say the least.

160

Julian moved in even further and stood behind the woman. She was on the tall side, slim with shoulder length mousey hair. And, apart from an apron fastened by a single knot tied at her lower back, completely naked. He studied her smallish, bare buttocks. Could you recognise a person from a part of the anatomy other than the face? Julian wondered, then realised he had spent too long wondering (and studying) and moved away. He walked to the other side, from where he could take a proper look at the man. Matching outfit, a kitchen apron and not much else. He was tall and slim too, but very muscular. He had long, slicked back black hair and perhaps a day's worth of stubble on his chin.

The woman was moving her mouth closer to the man's. She made a sound; not any attempt at real communication but some sort of purring, moaning gibberish. Julian frowned. She lifted up a long bare leg, raising the knee almost to chest height, and moved it slowly up and down, rubbing the inside against the man's torso and thigh. She did this repeatedly, apparently for the benefit of anyone in the kitchen who had missed it. Julian frowned. Having grasped the general idea of what was going on, he made a firm decision to leave. He took one last look at their aprons: bleached white, pristine, suitable wear for the kitchen of an award winning restaurant. They had both had their names embroidered, in flowing copper plate letters, in the top left corner of each apron. Julian read the man's name: Juan. On the woman's apron, embroidered in claret, was her name: Stephanie.

Julian felt dizzy and began to take quick, shallow breaths. He held on to the table for support. Right, well, perhaps he only had himself to blame. He almost ran out of the kitchen, determined to get out of that damned flat as fast as possible. He realised he was not running very far or fast; something was holding him back, bogging him down. No, he was out of breath but had only got half way down the corridor. What was going on? Someone had put a hand on his shoulder.

"Julian. I thought it was you." The voice was deep, formal but kind. The five words spoken exuded calm authority, as if the speaker owned not only the flat but the entire building and half the street too. Julian looked up and felt relieved. "Is everything okay? You look a little flustered," said the man. The tall frame was comfortingly familiar, the regular features benevolent, a messianic presence in this basement chamber of delights. "Come, let's sit down, have a chat. I've missed you. Being able to talk to someone on your own level is no easy matter these days." It was Julian's friend and benefactor, Richard Stein.

Relief flooded through his nervous system. "Yes, Mr Stein, that would be wonderful. Where..." Stein pointed at a large cream leather and wood sofa that Julian hadn't seen when he'd come in. Stein nodded and they both sat down.

"So Julian, how's the family these days?"

Julian hadn't told Stein anything about his private life. "Stephanie and I are doing fine, thank you for asking."

"It's a good thing to be married," Stein said, looking somewhat distant. "I was, once."

Julian wondered if he would ever be. "So, Mr Stein, how's life been treating you?" Stein nodded gently, confirming all was well. "I assume business is as healthy as ever?"

"It's okay right now, but I sense things will be getting a little tougher in the coming months. Some people will suffer."

"Yes I think you're right. I've noticed it – the economy turning down. House prices easing, people being short of cash and spending less."

"Hmm, yes," said Stein. "I had a rather unpleasant day today, actually."

"Oh, what happened?"

"I had to get rid of someone."

"It's never pleasant when you have to sack somebody."

"No, it's not nice," agreed Stein. "It can be pretty messy, actually." Stein reached into his tweed jacket pocket and pulled out a large stainless steel fountain pen. He slapped it slowly against his hand. It caught the light and Julian's eyes got the full force of the glint. "Sad to say, it's a messy business."

"So, er… will you be getting rid of a lot of people?"

Stein looked at him. "You know Julian, I've always said – and I told you this – it's hard to find talented individuals." Julian nodded. "But there's another problem. Sometimes a clever man can be, well, rather too clever for his own good."

"Yes. Right. In what sense, exactly?"

"I always feel safer trusting clever people. I mean, you don't want to hand your money over to some idiot, do you?" Julian shook his head. "But then, sometimes I end up regretting that trust. And I don't handle regret too well."

"Regret?"

"Be careful that your sharpest tool doesn't cut you first."

"That's very good, Mr Stein."

Stein turned to face him. The glare from his fountain pen shone into Julian's eyes. He squinted. "What should I do, Julian? A man is trying to steal from me. How do I stop it? Finish the deed, or the man? Which is the more complete act?" There was something unusual about that large fountain pen Stein kept slapping against his hand. Julian took a closer look at it. It wasn't a pen at all, but a knife with a sharp point and serrated edge.

He stood up. "Thank you, Mr Stein. It was a pleasure, I must say, but I really must be going now. Good night." He walked briskly to the front door and in a matter of seconds had left that basement forever.

Chapter 8

Lying in bed, in a state of pain and extreme dehydration, Julian refused to feel sorry for himself. He had known exactly what to expect. It is a fact widely acknowledged among drinkers that champagne produces the most merciless hangovers. Even his conscientious attempts to wash away the Bollinger with tumblerfuls of whiskey had produced no mitigating effect. Some virtuoso torturer-carpenter had clamped a vice to his face between his left temple and right lower jaw and was tightening it bit by bit. Each turn of the screw seemed to coincide perfectly with each new throb in his head.

Julian knew he had something very important to do today but couldn't remember what it was. He had noticed his smartphone flair up earlier, before he had properly woken up. Someone had sent him a text message, which might hopefully remind him what exactly the task was. Slowly and carefully, so as not to aggravate the cranial pounding, he reached for the phone and opened the message. "Hello Darling," it said, "I hope ur looking after yourself. I'm coming home tomorrow late. S. XX". Right, Stephanie coming home tomorrow evening meant he'd have one full day (and a bit of the next one) to get it done. But he still couldn't remember what he needed to do.

Last night. What had been strange about that party? And where had Sonia gone? Julian shrugged mentally. She was old enough to look after herself. He played with his smart phone to distract himself from the pain. How was business? How much of it was left? He opened the investor file. He frowned as commercial reality began to cause him agony of a different sort. Lots of numbers in red. Lots of money owing, most of it needing to be paid very shortly. Key clients having just deserted him. One big, generous client who was still with him... and who happened to be rather nasty when he wasn't making large investments... and whose cash was sitting in a numbered Swiss bank account with no traceable link to Julian. Of course, how could he be so forgetful? The task was obvious: he had a murder to carry out. The added complication (and this really was a bugger) was that he'd be doing it while hung over.

The problem was Julian had never killed anyone before and didn't really believe he could. Fraud was easy because you only had to look smart and tell a plausible story. Both those things played to his strengths. But murder was – how would you put it – a little too hands on? He'd have to be strong, though. Morally he knew exactly what he needed to do. The story made a perfect catechism: evil man makes money through crime. Said money is invested in a scheme which makes good (or at least better) people richer. To fund the payouts, the criminal must die. Sonia would definitely approve.

How do you do it? Morally, or technically? Julian didn't have much time and needed to get a few things sorted out. Firstly, all going well, by this time tomorrow Stein would be dead and Julian financially in the clear. But he would also be a murderer and he'd have to live with that. How would that affect his life from day to day? Would a dark shadow cloud his enjoyment of life, his leisurely mornings at Café Franz, his shopping trips and illicit kisses? But, on the other hand – so what? How many people's lives had Richard Stein destroyed, and how many had Julian improved? Now that his relative innocence had been confirmed, Julian knew his ales with Rob would continue to be supped with a spotless conscience.

Stein was a tall, fit man and that would make things harder from a practical perspective. That and Julian's raging headache (he had just swallowed four paracetamol tablets and was waiting for them to take effect). The best approach would be to hit Stein on the head with that heavy looking marble ashtray he had seen on his living room table. That would require Stein to be sitting down. Okay, Julian would find a way to arrange that. Get him talking, relaxed; he'd lean back in his seat, making things easier for Julian. What mood would Stein be in? Would he feel like chatting?

Julian had got out of bed and was walking around in his partially fastened silk dressing gown. He was beginning to feel better – a little light activity was clearly helping. One more brisk trot – the one up to Stein's house would be ideal – would get him right up to form, that perfect level of alertness which enabled him to be fully awake without any trace of nerves. Julian needed to be relaxed, conversational, hail fellow without being over the top. It occurred to him that he had never much minded the sight of blood. It was just another living tissue. Perhaps he might be pretty good at this? A businessman needed to have a large and diverse range of skills these days. And nobody knew that (or put it into practice) better than Stein himself.

The job would be a dirty one, but it still required a suit. Julian shifted several newish suits in his wardrobe out of way to get to a favourite old one. Favourite, that is, by way of its awfulness. He had bought it by mistake back in his engineering days but had never had the heart to give it away. After today, he decided, it was going to charity. He pulled it off the hanger – it was almost stuck to it – and took a good look at it. It had been dry cleaned before long term storage so there were no problems with stains. But oh my, that colour. Dark rust brown. An insalubrious mass of discarded, oxidised nails woven into a man's jacket and trousers. Perfectly suited for the task at hand. Julian would get spattered; it would be messy. But this suit wouldn't show it. And even better, that dark brown briefcase of his almost matched it.

He put it on and took a look at himself. It really wasn't all that bad, considering what was being asked of it. It was roomy and comfortable, allowing ample space for his shoulders to rotate and extend. He held his arms straight above his head and clasped his hands together. He thrust them down forcefully to waist height. Yes, that worked fine. The marble ashtray was all that was missing.

The walk up to Stein's house was leisurely, nurturing. Julian took deep, slow lungfuls of midday Summer air, a ten minute meditation on the move. He didn't care how he looked. He knew that was the first stage on the road to liberation – the second was due to take place in roughly twenty minutes. No thrill, no pleasurable shudder on seeing those palatial houses as he turned the corner into Hogarth Road. Those feelings somehow belonged in the past. He stood on the road in front of Stein's house, facing it. Right, now – Julian had a good look around – any sign of a Porsche? Or any other sports car, any vintage automotive beauty that had caused financial hardship but brought true pleasure and excitement to its owner? An owner who might just be a dedicated member of the police force, working extra hours without pay for his own satisfaction? An ambush by Toby at any point would be disastrous. Julian had been prepared to abandon everything and go home at the first sign of him. But today, no, he wasn't there. He had been out enjoying himself the night before. Yes, of course, he was sleeping in. The solid family saloons spread right across the driveway seemed to confirm that Toby and his automobile wouldn't be making an appearance.

Julian straightened himself, making the best of his suit, and rang Stein's doorbell. Stein answered, wearing a dark brown dressing gown with green embroidery. His pyjamas underneath were black silk. For a moment Julian was struck by how much like him Stein looked. Taller and more severe featured, true, but... surely he was looking at himself in the doorway, twenty years from now? "Mr Stein. Good morning," he said.

Stein nodded in recognition. "Julian? Hello."

"Sorry to surprise you like this, but I thought I'd drop by and update you on what's been going on. With your investment."

Stein looked at Julian's suit and frowned. "The investment? Ah, right, yes." He frowned again. "I thought you were just going to send me the monthly statements, right?"

"Of course, you'll get those as a matter of course. I just thought – well, if you have a moment or two, I could give you more of an in depth summary."

Stein held the door open. "Well, you may as well come in."

"I do hope I'm not interrupting anything, Mr–"

"No, not at all." Stein cleared his throat and smoothed down his dressing gown. "Please do come in and sit down. You know the way. It's actually good to see you again, Julian. Haven't had much intelligent conversation all week, to be honest."

Julian was happy to partake in intelligent conversation, but today, sadly, it would be rather brief. "Thanks Mr Stein. I'll do my best to provide some." Julian sat down and looked at the coffee table. Yes, that grey marble ashtray was in the same place. He pushed it a millimetre or two with his index finger. And yes, it was heavy. He had a quick look around the room. There was something else, a new item that hadn't been there last time. What, exactly? He looked at each shelf, seat, table top – what new silhouette was his peripheral vision picking up? A photograph frame, of course, perching rather temporarily on a lower bookshelf. Silver, modern, minimalist with a black and white picture of a man in his thirties. He was dressed in a flannel grey jacket and dark tie. Very smart. Julian knew straight away that it was Stein's son.

Stein sat down in his armchair, positioning himself at a right angle to Julian. He raised his eyebrows and tilted his head. "So?" His mouth made the tiniest of smiles. He looked pointedly at Julian's awful suit, as if to emphasise how polite he was being by not saying anything.

"Well, I thought I'd give you an update on markets in general," said Julian, "you know, the global financial situation. Did you hear about ITCB?"

"Oh yes, I did. Very unfortunate. You don't often hear about banks actually collapsing, do you? Well, not nowadays."

"I don't want to worry you, but things could be getting a little volatile from here onwards. The economy turning down, that sort of thing."

"Okay. Yes, I see how that might be a risk. How would that affect this investment?"

"You see, Mr. Stein, that's the beauty of what we're doing. We're pretty much immune from whatever the economy does. Your three percent per month is pretty safe."

"Yes, that's what I thought." Stein looked slightly puzzled, as if to say, was that all you wanted to talk about? Damn, this wasn't really working. Julian needed to get him relaxed, in a mood to sit back in his armchair and chat about everything and nothing; that magical state you enter when conversation with an old friend gets into full swing. Julian wanted to be there with him.

"So, how's the nightclub business?"

"Fine. Yes, can't say I've noticed much of a slowdown. Not yet." His eyes wandered towards his wristwatch. "Actually, Julian, if there wasn't any–"

"Is that your son? That young man in the picture."

"Yes. Yes, it is."

"I thought so. He looks exactly like you."

"Yes, well, that photo is up there on that shelf on and off. Sometimes I shove it back in the drawer. Other times I have to take it out, just stare at it for a while." He looked Julian in the eye. "Do you have children, Julian?"

"No, not yet. I'm due to get married soon, so let's see."

Stein nodded. "Well, it's probably of no interest to you anyway. You're still young."

"No, not at all. Tell me, how often do you see your son?" Julian stood up, walked over to the bookshelf and picked up the photograph frame. He studied the familiar facial features. "Are you two close?"

"We were when he was very young. After that we never really had much in common."

"No?"

"He wanted to waste his life. Music."

"But you like music, don't you, Mr. Stein?" Julian walked over to the hi-fi and looked at the classical compact discs in Stein's collection. Just as he had remembered them: not one out of place. Holding the photograph frame under his arm, he pulled out the disc of Mahler's *Resurrection* symphony, inserted it into the CD player and skipped tracks one to four. He pressed 'play' for track five, the fifth movement. The finale.

Stein watched him with interest. "Mahler?"

"Yes, I love him, too." The music began. A huge clash of cymbals – quite startlingly rendered by Stein's first rate hi-fi system – then foreboding, uncertain, funereal strains. Julian stood still and listened. The grimness gave way to hopeful fanfares which descended once again into tension and darkness. Julian looked at Stein. He was sitting back in the armchair, listening carefully. He was spellbound. Julian walked over to him and handed him the photograph frame – which Stein took silently – while Julian simultaneously picked up the ashtray with his other hand.

"Wonderful, isn't it?" said Stein. "Life would be unbearable without Mahler." He looked down at the photograph and studied it.

Julian nodded. The music was now dramatic, heroically conflict ridden. Maybe hope, in the form of a charming melody rising out of pain, now stood some chance? "So your son was a musician?"

"Yes, but he couldn't make much of a career out of it. I didn't help. I never encouraged him much."

"Well I wanted to be a writer once. Didn't get very far with it. What does he do now?"

"He had a lot of problems. I blame myself for everything that went wrong."

"What happened?" Julian was holding the ashtray to one side so Stein couldn't see it. It was heavier than he had thought and his hand was aching, but the music provided a welcome distraction from the pain.

Stein sighed. "I really think we were just two very different sorts of people. I never really got the artistic personality type. He wasn't interested in the business and I must say that upset me." He tightened his facial features, determined not to betray any of the emotions his words might induce. "He had his problems, too."

"Problems? What sort of problems?" Julian focussed his mind on the music once again. The finale had entered its final section. The choir sang an optimistic theme, tenors and sopranos set on their decisive march to the jubilant end.

"Well, call it the creative soul, I don't know. He was a bit unstable."

"And what happened to him?"

"He had a problem with drugs. He was an addict. Drugs. Ha!" he exclaimed, "the sheer irony of it."

"Irony?"

"Something I've never tolerated, drugs. Not for an instant. My son was weak, that's all."

"Did you two ever... make it up? Reconcile?"

"He died two years ago. Aged thirty-two. Overdose." Stein sat perfectly still, looking down at the photograph. "I should have tried harder."

It was as Julian had known right from the start. The inherent impossibility of a great man passing on his legacy had proven itself. What would he do in the same position? One couldn't rely on progeny living up to expected standards. The heir had to be selected. Or better still, self-appointed. "Sorry, Mr. Stein" he said, very quietly.

The music had quickened its tempo. It was louder, triumphant, marching home in a blaze of glory. It grew stronger, more forceful. Final victory was in sight. Julian swung the ashtray up above his head with one arm and raised the other to hold it in place with both hands. He had assumed a religious pose, arms stretched out to heaven, holding his offering aloft. Without moving, Stein looked up at him. The choir, organ and orchestra were now in a state of ecstasy, proudly announcing that the dead would be raised, that the kingdom of heaven was descending to earth.

Julian closed his eyes and swung the corner of the ashtray down onto Stein's head with all his strength. He opened them and saw a small spurt of crimson rise from the top of his head. After a second or two it gave way to a thick, darker flow of blood. Stein slumped forward, then fell to the side. He remained in the same position, that of an intoxicated body passed out after too much indulgence. Julian knew that Stein, like himself, rarely touched alcohol.

What exactly are you supposed to do now? Julian became aware of the strange silence, the emptiness in the room. The symphony had ended and the CD player was whirring, preparing to switch to standby mode and dim its green LED display. He stared at Stein, curious at how the long limbs were all perfectly balanced in that position. He grabbed one wrist and attempted to feel for a pulse, using the overlong jacket sleeves to shield his fingers. All good killers wait for the pulse to die away, don't they? He felt nothing, but in truth wasn't sure exactly where the pulse was located. How dead was Stein on a scale of one to ten? Julian was scared of anything below ten. He imagined Stein snorting, growling and getting up, lunging at him in a fury. He stepped back a few inches. Right, at least he wasn't breathing. Just wait five full minutes. No movement, no breathing and it's probably all clear.

The minute hand of his watch traversed the angle required. Okay. Stein really was dead. Julian looked at his hands. Not too much blood; just a little spattering on the outer edges, now almost dry. The off-white cuffs of his shirt were untouched; the jacket sleeves that hung half way down his hands had made sure of that. He entered the hallway and walked over to the kitchen – large, ultra-modern design, and clearly never used for cooking – to wash his hands. He did a thorough job, using a strong jet of very cold water and nothing else. His hands burned with cold. He turned the tap off and shook them, restoring some feeling to them. He tore off a piece of kitchen towel from a stylish metallic dispenser attached to the wall and walked back to the living room.

One corner of the marble ashtray was stained deep red with dried blood, some lighter streaks running off it. He picked it up using the piece of kitchen towel and opened his briefcase with the other hand. He dropped both ashtray and paper towel into the case's largest compartment and shut it, refastening the buckle. He picked up the briefcase. It felt heavy, but not unduly so, and the ashtray inside seemed to have assumed a stable position; there was no sliding or rattling.

He looked again at Stein. He tried to imagine what the police would think when, in a matter of several hours or days, they would examine the sprawled body of this tall, lean man, deprived of his cultured, prosperous life in the prime of his late middle years. They knew he was a criminal, a major one. Clearly some disgruntled business associate must have done this to him. How thoroughly would they investigate? Did murdered murderers rank lower down? Surely the real victims should get priority. Some blood, now dried, had trickled onto Stein's face, giving him the appearance of a knocked out boxer. Julian imagined that he had been a pretty good fighter in his day, and felt grateful that he'd killed him instantly. He shuddered at the thought that he might have had to grapple with him. He felt a small throb in his head – no, he hadn't taken enough paracetamol – and, picking up the briefcase, decided to get out of Stein's house as quickly as possible.

The way out would be made easier by the parked cars. The boxy family saloons were arranged in the front drive like a group of small islands, forming a string that led all the way to the street. This provided Julian with a perfect sequence of bases to hide behind, giving him the ability to jump to the next one when all was clear (he could see the street through each car's side windows). He closed the front door softly and made a dash for the first car. He crouched, panting slightly. He took a good look at the street. Okay, he had a clear run. Julian hopped, skipped, almost flew from behind one car to the next until he was on the street, walking quickly away from Stein's house towards the main road on the hill. He sighed, elated, and swung his briefcase back and forth.

Someone shouted at him from far behind. "Jonathan. Hey! Julian I mean, slow down!" Julian stopped, the suddenness causing the weight in his briefcase to jolt forward. He turned round. It was Rob running towards him, looking surprisingly dapper in a navy blue blazer and jeans. Had he lost weight? "Hey Jules. My god, I remember that suit. Didn't think I'd see it ever again!"

"H-hi Rob," said Julian. He slowed down his breathing. He wasn't going to panic. "Good to see you." Of course. Rob had recently moved into Hogarth Road and was renting a room four houses down from Stein's. How bloody convenient.

Rob pointed at Stein's house. "I see you know that old bloke. Strange man, a bit sinister I think. Polite enough though."

Julian was in control. There was absolutely no risk of an asthma attack. "Yes, he's a client of mine, actually. Just had some business to catch up with."

Rob pointed at the briefcase. "Well he must keep you busy. That briefcase is stuffed to bursting."

"Yes, he's pretty demanding."

Rob looked closely at Julian's face. "You cut yourself shaving. You really must've been in a rush this morning! You've got some blood just there." Rob pointed at his own chin.

Julian wiped it away with his finger. "Rob," he said, putting a hand on his shoulder, "I haven't seen you in a while. Why don't we have a drink? The Railway's literally a few minutes away."

"Well, actually– " Rob appeared to be thinking. He looked away. "Yes, sure, why not? I was heading up to the high street anyway."

"Really?" Julian kept his hand firmly on Rob's shoulder.

"Yes, to the bookshop."

Julian couldn't imagine Rob in a bookshop, but wherever Rob was going, Julian was going with him. Long before Rob would ever get a chance to browse the shelves, select his book, leaf through the pages and take it to the cashier he would be dead. Julian had about ten minutes to get the job done. That's if they walked slowly. Luckily Rob had short legs and never made any attempt to rush. Okay, that was a safe ten minutes of leisurely strolling. Enough time, but only just. Julian had an instrument of death in his briefcase that had already proven its worth, but he quickly realised it couldn't be used again. Not that luring Rob into the wooded area between here and the high street on some silly pretext would be a problem. The problem was that two people who had a connection to Julian would both have the same shaped head wound. No, that idea was a non-starter. There was a lot of traffic on the main road. That's it. He would push Rob into the path of a speeding car (they all went too fast on that stretch anyway). Perfect.

Apart from having to think quickly, Julian knew the next few minutes would be emotionally wrenching. Rob was Julian's best friend, in fact his only real one. He was going to howl with sorrow inside but not flinch from committing the act. And actually... *best friend* – what did that mean? It was just an overused phrase, one that Julian increasingly couldn't attach any sentiment to. It was all merely words now, a list of precise steps to follow, simple verbal logic. He tried momentarily to focus on his feelings. What were they? Just mild alarm coupled with determination; that was all.

Rob looked at Julian's hand on his shoulder. It had been there a little too long. Julian gave it a playful squeeze and patted Rob on the back. "Come on then. A nice walk should help us build up a thirst." Rob nodded and followed. Julian paced himself. Walking much slower than usual, Rob was able to keep up with him without any visible effort. "So Rob, how's work these days?"

"There's not much of it, frankly. I'm working out my three month notice period."

"Ah yes. Those redundancies."

"Yeah, the company's pretty screwed. Not much for me to do at the office. I'm just sitting around."

So his prospects weren't good. Knowing that might, possibly, make things a tiny bit easier for Julian. They had practically nothing in common nowadays. "Hence your new found interest in literature?"

"Yes! It does help pass the time. I'll tell you something, Julian – never thought I'd enjoy it so much."

"What are you reading?"

"Those books you used to be really into. All those Russian writers."

Now, who might have influenced Rob in that direction? What exactly was going on between him and Sonia? Julian looked closely at him. Yes, his dress sense had markedly improved. He had never spent money on clothes before. And books? Something was happening between those two. But it was impossible to say what exactly. Then again, it wasn't all that straightforward to guess what Sonia's taste in men was. Or whether she actually had any sort of preference. Sonia had feelings for Julian; surely she did? After last night? Yes, without a doubt, there was something there; something he felt was vital, an insurance policy should things fall apart with Stephanie (and god knows, how close had he come to that?) Could Rob mess things up, destroy Julian's delicious romantic sideline? Rob had no idea what was at stake. His cheerful bumbling, his sheer likeability, could spoil everything Julian had done to impress Sonia. No, dispatching Rob would be quite easy after all. Julian saw all the steps clearly now: the speeding car, the sudden push onto the street after tripping him up, the screeching brakes, the ensuing mayhem, his own shock and sorrow. There were now only a few more minutes to go. He breathed deeply and kept calm.

They had turned onto the main road and were walking slowly uphill. Cars that had seemed sluggish and silent a quarter of a mile away roared and hissed as they sped past him. No driver was paying any attention to speed restrictions. This was just a pleasant suburban thoroughfare, a little too long, straight and devoid of

181

speed bumps to pay any real attention to. Time for the driver's mind to drift and his foot to rest heavily on the accelerator.

"Let's cross here," said Julian. They turned to face the road and walked right to the edge of the pavement. Julian placed his hand in front of Rob's waist to instruct him to wait and be careful. Julian could see a large, black BMW in the distance, its double radiator grille grinning like a panther ready to pounce on its dinner. First silence, then a soft woosh; it came closer and... yes, now it was just the right distance away. The driver was a thick set, balding man of middle eastern appearance. His mind seemed to be miles away. Julian put his right leg just in front of Rob's left, leaned back and pushed him onto the road with both hands. In an instant the driver's expression turned to one of horror. He slammed his foot down on the brake pedal, sliding downwards in his seat as he pulled on the steering wheel for extra force. The screeching was very slight (it was an expensive car) but the stationery wheels scraped along the road for several feet. Too late – Rob was launched into the air like a large pillow thrown across a child's bedroom. He landed on his back, his head hitting the road a fraction of a second later.

The driver stopped, switched on the car's blinkers and got out. He rushed over to Julian. The driver looked terror stricken. "He – he just suddenly jumped out! What – I mean, there was no warning!"

Julian put on his horrified expression, studying the driver's face for guidance. "Oh my god. I just have no idea why he did that."

"What was he thinking?"

"I can't imagine. He was acting quite strangely today, but – my god." He motioned towards Rob and he and the driver walked quickly to where Rob was sprawled on the road.

"I wasn't speeding, not at all. I swear, I was doing thirty-five miles per hour. Absolutely. I'm always very careful on this road. I drive very carefully."

"Can you call the ambulance, please? My phone battery's dead." In fact, Julian had no phone on his person. The duties earlier on had meant it needed to be left at home. Location identification would have been fatal.

"Sure." As the driver made the phone call, a family hatchback sluggishly drove round the stopped BMW and continued, at an even slower pace – lingering to the point of indecency – around Rob and returned to the correct side of the road for its onward journey. Julian took a closer look at him. He was lying on his back, his legs slightly apart. One knee was bent. His head rocked slowly from side to side, the mouth was partially open, the eyes had rolled back in their sockets. Julian shuddered.

"I just called nine-nine-nine," the driver panted, "the ambulance should be about ten minutes."

"Can I take your contact details?"

"Sure. And look, really, I was doing thirty-five, you know, exactly thirty-five miles per hour." He gave Julian his business card: *Mr Mo Syed, B.Sc., UK retail, import/export and international trading.* Julian put it in his pocket. "Was – is he a friend of yours?"

"Yes, a close friend."

"I'm so sorry." Mr Syed put a hand on Julian's upper arm, then seemed to regret what he had just said and removed his hand. He looked down at the ground.

The ambulance arrived, having continuously flashed its blue light and wailed the entire length of the almost empty road. Two paramedics unfurled a stretcher from the back and performed some basic medical checks on Rob. They questioned Mr Syed for a minute or two.

A small and efficient fair haired ambulanceman approached Julian. "Luckily he's still alive. Made of some pretty strong stuff I reckon. He's breathing – slowly – but he's unconscious."

"Will he be okay?"

"I really can't tell you at this stage. We're stabilising him right now but we'll know much more after doing some tests at the hospital. Likely several bones broken along with the head injury." Julian recited Rob's personal and contact details (including that godforsaken new address) and the medic jotted them down as quickly as he spoke.

Mr Syed and the ambulance both drove off – the BMW cautiously, the ambulance speedily. Julian stood still and held his breath until both vehicles were out of sight and inaudible.

What was friendship, anyway? What did it boil down to? Merely a permanent quest to recreate the comfortable and familiar, a sort of deliberate striving for mediocrity. The same enjoyable, humorous, salacious conversations trotted out time after time, as the venue and occasion varied minutely: what girls are wearing these days discussed over drinks, politics argued about at dinner, hamburger fragments spat out while deciding which supermodel was one's favourite (and how thoroughly she deserved to take over from the goddess mistakenly chosen last month). How does this habit called friendship start? From a sharp point in the void at which loneliness and chemistry coincide. Friends constantly crave to experience that moment again. Entire social lives are arranged (and lifetimes wasted) around attempting to recreate something that really couldn't have meant anything in the first place.

Julian exhaled, coughed and walked home slowly, taking care not to swing the briefcase too vigorously.

Chapter 9

It wasn't much to look at right now with its dusty floors and whitewashed windows, but Julian thought the premises they had just entered had great potential. Neither too large nor small, on the ground floor and with a decent ceiling height and first rate location on the high street, it would make a perfect home for Stephanie's new restaurant venture. The five of them – Steph, Allegra, Marek and the commercial estate agent were with him – had all had the same reaction on first seeing it: a sort of "ah, yes, there's definitely something about this place." Stephanie and Allegra immediately began pacing around. Looking up and down, they examined the interior features and the previous owners' fittings, frequently oohing and aahing, occasionally frowning.

They looked at each other and nodded. Yes, they were convinced.

Marek was having a good look around, too. Julian saw him doing the calculations in his head – tins of paint, spare brushes, other workers to hire – and saw a smile grow steadily on his face. Things were beginning to slow down a bit in the house refurbishment market (he was currently without work) and this assignment would provide some welcome funds. He pulled out a small writing pad and, moving his lips only very slightly, wrote down a series of notes in what could only have been Polish. Julian glanced discreetly at the squiggles and tried to guess which ones symbolised plaster, putty, cigarettes, masking tape, beer.

Stephanie walked up to Julian and put her arms round his shoulders. She moved her face close to his and whispered, "Thank you." She kissed him gently. Julian, kissing her back, felt proud and content, that sense of achievement that true family men, the providers, should have the right to feel. What had he been through to get this far? To secure for the woman he loved exactly what she desired? Stephanie would never find out what had been necessary. As her husband-to-be he would make sure of that above all else. Allegra was looking at them both, a small, tender smile on her face. Julian knew she wished them both well.

"Must say, it looks like the missus has fallen for this gaff in a big way. Don't you reckon?" The estate agent was in his mid-twenties, taller than they usually were, and very enthusiastically cockney for a young middle class man raised in north London. "You're not going to let her down, are you?"

"Thanks Dan, this is a great find. How long has it been on the market?"

"Only one viewer before you and that was yesterday. I wouldn't hang around if I were you."

"Okay, we'll go for it. At the asking price. Can you email me the lease and deposit terms?" Stephanie squeezed him, her eyes shining.

"I think," said Allegra, "we should set up an open plan kitchen. We could actually have it right here in the middle, maybe partially sectioned off by some glass or bare brickwork."

"That's a super idea," said Stephanie. "Stylish, and it'd be a great way to maximise seating too. I think we're going to be packing those diners in."

"And keeping them slim, don't forget".

Julian was glad to see them getting along so well. Good friends were priceless, individuals to be cherished throughout life. He thought about his last few days and how close he had come to losing his closest companion for good. The things fate had forced him to do! If only Rob had gone for his walk a few minutes earlier or later. Or had chosen to live somewhere else, even just a few streets away. Luck could be a rotten shrew. But on second thoughts: Rob was still alive. Unable to speak or remember, but still breathing. Maybe things had a way of turning out for the best after all.

"Keep an eye on these two," he said to Marek, pointing at the two women. "Tell them what's realistic, how much their ideas are going to cost. Just to make sure their feet stay on the ground." Marek smiled and nodded. Julian put his hand on his shoulder for a second and walked towards the door. He had a couple of appointments to keep that day.

Julian lay back in the grey leather dentist's chair and relaxed. He deserved a chance to take it easy for a while, even in this unlikely position. Sunil's face was a mere foot from his. He was working inside Julian's mouth with a long, spindly cotton swab, busily applying a cold gel-like substance to his gums. Julian studied his small moustache and noticed how much greyer it had become since their last meeting.

Sunil finished, stood up and walked over to the worktop. "Well, that's the gum protection applied. I've just got to mix this next paste up and I'll be right back. By the way, what convinced you to go for it in the end?"

Julian spoke quietly, trying not to move his lips too much. The cold substance was burning his gums. "Just thought I'd bite the bullet and go for it. I had a bit of quiet patch on the client front. And what better way to use up some free time? Every man should get his teeth whitened."

"That's what I say. Unless you happen to have exceptional oral hygiene and never drink tea, coffee or red wine. Not most of my patients."

"It's sort of like spring cleaning. A phase change, you know, a new chapter."

"Really? Can't think what you'd need to change. Things seem to going great for you, Julian."

"What makes you say that?"

"Well, successful financier, great house, beautiful girlfriend. What else can I say? Me" – he looked around his dental studio – "I'm just surviving these days. It's really impressive how the downturn doesn't seem to have affected you."

"Thanks for the praise, Sunil. But to be frank, I'm tired of this game, downturn or not. Look– "

"Yes?" Sunil was walking towards him with a rose coloured clear plastic gum shield in each hand. Each pink receptacle was filled with a thick grey-white paste.

"This may come as a surprise but I want to retire soon. Maybe to travel for a while, or help Stephanie full time. She's starting a restaurant, you know."

"Oh yes? What kind of restaurant?"

"Indian. Low carb cuisine, so it's not so fattening."

"Sounds like a winner. I'll probably become a regular."

"So Sunil, I'm thinking of returning all investor funds by the end of the month. You've still got a hundred grand with me, and of course the interest on that. I'll have to work it out." Paying Sunil's original deposit back would use up the last dregs of Stein's legacy.

"Right. Well this is pretty sudden. Why are you leaving the business?"

"I can't give you an exact reason. Just a feeling that I've had enough. You may have heard that old gambler's saying: when you're winning, quit the casino?"

"Casino?"

"I just meant I fancy doing something totally different with my life. A new direction. I feel I owe it to myself. And Stephanie."

Sunil sighed. "Okay. You've got to do what you feel you must. I'd love to talk you out of it but it looks like you've made your mind up." He looked at the pink plastic dental shields he was holding. "Someday I'll retire from this. Travel the world. Not visit the in-laws in Chandigarh every other year, I mean really travel." He walked over to Julian and fitted the shields securely inside his already open mouth.

Julian closed his mouth, then his eyes and drifted off.

He felt refreshed and relaxed. His mouth tingled slightly. The walk from Sunil's new dental studio (the one that was struggling) to the tube station – somewhere near the southernmost rungs of the Northern line – was a mere five minutes, enough to get a sense of the young, rapidly gentrifying neighbourhood. He thought of Sonia and how this would be the perfect location for her first flat. The weather was good, too: sunny, but not obtrusively so. The recently refurbished tube station had a gleaming white entrance and ticket hall which belied the very long, dark and rather dirty descent by escalator onto the platform. Julian was about to spend an hour or so at this depth, travelling many, many stops northwards to his own salubrious corner of northwest London.

The platform was very quiet. It was at least two hours before the evening rush was due to start, and the handful of people who had slipped out of work early or didn't have a job paced up and down slowly and guiltily. Some of them were people just like Julian, he felt: creative, entrepreneurial, not suited to regular hours.

The rumbling crescendo and final climactic woosh of the train arriving seemed louder than usual. Fewer people on the platform to absorb the sound. He sat down in an almost empty carriage (he had several to choose from) and looked around. He noticed how messy it was. Lots of morning newspapers – the free, tacky variety – littered the entire seating area. He found a copy that wasn't too dog eared and began reading. He had done something in the past few days that most would consider newsworthy. Would it have made it into the papers yet? He flicked dismissively through the stories about house prices and pop starlets until, on page five, he saw that two column inches had been allocated to a story under the heading *London businessman found killed in own home:*

Richard Stein, a successful north London businessman, was discovered dead in the living room of his own home in Hogarth Road, Hampstead Garden Suburb on Thursday, 23rd June. He had sustained serious injuries to his skull from a heavy object. His housekeeper, Mrs Vlada Volodchenko of Norwood, South London, discovered his body after letting herself in and immediately contacted the police. Stein, 62, had built up a string of nightclubs and casinos throughout the city and was regarded as a prominent figure in the industry.

Julian imagined he should feel something after reading that, but was only aware of an oddly gnawing emptiness. Stein probably wouldn't be missed too much, but Julian had felt a bond with him. He and Stein were special, so similar to each other, both different from the herd. Julian realised the mantle had indeed been passed on, but was he living up to it? Stein had persevered until his dying day but Julian – he cringed physically – was giving up, making life easy for himself.

How long had he been on the train? It was well and truly in (or rather, under) north London, just a handful of stops from Julian's. But an idea had occurred to him. When the train stopped at the next station, he got off. At street level he was a few hundred yards south of the Railway pub. He walked north (which happened to be uphill on this stretch of the high street) and entered a shabby looking, family owned all-purpose grocery store. The man behind the counter thought he recognised Julian and nodded without exerting his atrophied smile muscles. Four minutes later Julian emerged, carrying a large brown paper bag with reinforced handles. Something heavy was inside it.

He turned right off the high street and followed a steep descent through a well-manicured park with plenty of wooden benches. After that came a large parking lot. It belonged to a vast fifteen story glass and concrete structure, that controversial icon of nineteen sixties architecture: the Royal Northwest Hospital, London.

Julian entered and walked up to the reception desk. A middle aged woman looked up at him. "Good afternoon. I've come to visit Rob Jollison. Which room is he in?"

"Jolli-i-son," echoed the woman as she typed the name into the computer terminal. "Okay, it's family only at the moment."

"I'm his cousin."

"His room's on corridor 2B on the tenth floor."

"Thank you." Julian had spent time in hospital twice in his life. Once as a child after a particularly severe asthma attack. The second time was at the age of seventeen when he had contracted meningitis. It'd been diagnosed quickly, thankfully. He noticed how the smell of a modern hospital, though a marked improvement from years ago, was still unmistakeably clinical.

The nurse on duty up on the tenth floor gave him a tissue face mask and plastic apron to put on. She led him to Rob's room and told him there was no particular need to be quiet, and that "talking to him will help". Rob had a feeding tube inserted through his nose and a sensor wrapped around one finger. Other than that he was breathing slowly and deeply, looking totally peaceful, somewhat like a large baby taking his afternoon nap.

Julian rested the paper bag at the foot of the bed and pulled out the heavy object. It was a one litre brown glass bottle of ale. He prised off the cap using the edge of the bedside table, raised the bottle and took a sip. "Cheers, Rob." He placed the bottle on the table. His voice became a tight, strained whisper. "And sorry. I'm so terribly sorry." He pushed open the door and quietly walked out.

When Julian got home he was greeted – hugged tightly, in fact – by a still excited Stephanie. "Tonight, Julian," she said, "you and I are going out. My treat. I've booked a table at *La Gazza Ladra*. Do you know it?

"Okay, that sounds really nice. Yes, I've walked past it a few times."

"We haven't done anything romantic in ages. It's just been all work and no play – for both of us."

"Steph, you are so right. Great idea." He gave her a little wink. "But Italian food. That's pretty heavy on the carbs, don't you think?"

"Even I deserve a break every now and then." She nudged him, grinning, and took his hand. A taxi had arrived and was waiting for them.

The cabbie dropped them off right outside the restaurant where the outdoor whicker tables and chairs had been arranged, positioned for maximum space usage. It was very busy. Midsummer evening, warm but not humid, pink tinged twilight at the perfect level – none of this had been lost on the locals. "Table for two at eight booked for Stephanie?" she said to the maitresse d'. The waiter standing next to her was the same one who had served Julian when he had been there with Sonia. He gave him a brief nod and smile (nothing too obvious) and led him and Stephanie to their table. It was right next to the one Julian, Sonia and Rob had been sitting at. They sat down and Julian looked at the people on that table for his amusement: a quartet of elderly ladies on their final coffee of the night. One of them had an empty glass of brandy in front of her.

"Would you like to start with a drink?" asked the waiter, "some champagne, perhaps?"

"Oh yes, why not?" Stephanie seemed even more ebullient than earlier. Julian remembered his hangover from a few days ago and resolved to sip one glass very slowly for the rest of the evening.

"Excellent, ma'am. A glass of champagne each, or would you prefer a bottle?" He opened the wine menu and pointed at the short list of champagnes.

"I think I'd like a bottle of this," said Stephanie, pointing at the non-vintage Moët. The waiter nodded vigorously to acknowledge her excellent taste and rushed off to fetch it. Stephanie looked into Julian's eyes. She held his fingers tightly. "Now," she said, "why don't you tell me what you've been up to. I really should be paying more attention to you."

Julian studied Stephanie's face, the face of the woman for whom he had changed himself into someone he didn't know. He felt nothing but weariness as he refamiliarised himself with the blue grey eyes, the small, straight nose, the lightest dusting of freckles – all of which had once thrilled him. "Nothing really. Just the usual."

"I was away for a full week. You had an entire seven days of freedom. And you sit here and tell me 'just the usual'?"

"I wouldn't call it freedom as such. I was catching up with work. Pensions administration, some investment related stuff."

"When I came home you had dark circles under your eyes. You looked as if you'd been hitting the town every night."

"Well perhaps I went out for a drink once or twice."

"With that Rob character, I'll bet?" Stephanie had never met Rob but seemed to hold some strong opinions about him. "Trust him to lead you astray."

"Yes, with Rob a couple of times. So what? And please stop thinking he's a bad influence on me. If anything it's the other way round." Julian's voice sounded harsh and irritated. Its tone surprised him.

"It's just that he's never really made much of his life. I mean, he's still–"

"Just stop having a go at him all the time, okay?" Julian almost shouted. A couple of the old ladies turned their heads to look.

Stephanie's face softened. "All right. I know he's a good friend of yours." She put her hand on his clenched fist, covering it. "And that must mean something." She smiled – happily, sweetly. "We're here to celebrate, aren't we Julian? Here's to us. Santé!"

Julian raised his champagne flute and clinked Stephanie's. "Absolutely. To us, Steph. And your restaurant."

"Yes, I've been so excited all day. But you know what? There's someone else we should be toasting." Julian made a quizzical face. "I've been thinking about this. Since when did things start going really well for us?"

"We've been doing okay for some time. Don't you think?"

"Sure, but I meant when was the turning point? I think I can recall the exact day your business really started hitting the big time."

"When was that?"

"I just remember that gorgeous green letter paper. That wealthy new client of yours. Stein. Robert... Stein. That's his name, isn't it?"

"No, he didn't sign up in the end." Julian had to be careful. Stephanie's memory was patchy, but vivid. "He thought about it, then decided not to go ahead."

"Oh. Okay." Stephanie looked puzzled, and also a little annoyed. Her cleverness had hit a dead end. "But you're definitely doing something right. That briefcase of yours is bulging." It was sitting under the desk in his study. Had Stephanie wandered in there?

Julian spluttered a little into his glass and cleared his throat. Yes, he'd have to sort that out. "You know how thorough you need to be with the paperwork these days." But there was nothing to worry about. He had locked the briefcase.

"Have you decided on your starters?" asked the waiter. They nodded and ordered: Stephanie asked for the bruschetta and Julian, after some deliberation, decided he was in the mood for the baby octopus.

"I've got so many ideas for the restaurant," said Stephanie, "that prioritising is going to be the biggest problem for me. Allegra's going to be a great help – I love her suggestions. Don't you think she and I make a great team?" Julian nodded. "I've projected our takings. I actually went into some quite detailed figures on the train back from Hampshire. I think," – she looked up and to the side – "we could easily take ten thousand a week."

"Revenue or profit?" mumbled Julian. He focussed again on Stephanie's faint freckles but they failed to hold his attention. Behind her sat a woman in her late twenties, long limbed and elegant. She had a dark brunette bob, glossy and expensively coiffed. She was talking to two men sitting at her table: one slightly older than her, the other much more so. They seemed transfixed by her. She sat back in the whicker seat, cross legged, very cool. What had they all planned for later, Julian wondered?

She was taller and older than Sonia but composed of the same essences. A taxi – or more likely, a limousine hired for the night – would come to pick the three of them up after the final grappas and sambuccas had been downed. They would all be feeling deliciously tipsy, adventurous; the girl would be laughing sweetly, pubescently as the men cackled, flirting with them just enough to keep them interested while not allowing any hands to explore too far. They would pass shop windows in the smarter parts of town. She would point to shoes, dresses, and jewellery and express the desire for a beau who thought she was special enough to deserve them. The men would laugh, poking fun at her taste, but take note of what she wanted. She, for her part, would be listening attentively (how the eyes would widen, the lips make an O) to their tales of daring, of bargains agreed and profits booked in the exciting world of convertible bond sales. The more elderly of the two men would do the decent thing and tire first. The two surviving revellers would drop him off at his central pied à terre, leaving them free to talk more deeply about affairs of the heart. Arriving at the younger's very understated pad, she would slip her high heels off at the door, curse them for the pain they always cause her and sashay into the reception. In a single smooth move she would be lying full length on the long leather sofa. "Do you have anything to drink? Champagne would be just perfect." And so the night would begin in earnest.

Stephanie was gripping his fist, tighter than ever before. "I see you as a sort of role model, Julian. Imagine if I became as successful as you. Wouldn't that be absolutely super? I'm definitely going to name a dish after you. Whichever one you choose as your favourite."

The weather was so perfect that they decided to walk home. Fingers intertwined, their gait was a slow half stroll, half goosestep. They didn't say anything but frequently looked at each other, sometimes smiling, now and then stifling a giggle. Stephanie looked like a young woman who had everything she needed – and most of what she wanted – in life, at least for now.

"Don't you ever get excited, Julian?"

"About what?"

"Just life in general. And us. Our future."

"I suppose that's something to look forward to, yes."

"You suppose?" she pouted.

"No, definitely, I have a good feeling about things."

"I'm with an engineer, I know. Cold and logical. No feelings, just numbers."

"That's a little harsh, don't you think?"

"Maybe. But one thing I will say about you guys. You're so reliable. Where would I be without you?" She hugged him as they continued walking.

Before they reached their front door Julian caught sight of Toby and his Porsche in their front drive. Judging from his slow, absent minded pacing, he had been waiting for them for a while. The doors of his sports car had been left wide open on account of the weather.

"What a gorgeous car," said Stephanie to Julian. "Do you know the owner?"

Julian walked up to Toby and slapped him on the shoulder. "Good to see you. What brings you up here?"

"Hi Julian, well," – he smiled joylessly and sighed – "where shall I start? There've been some developments, let's put it that way. Not all bad, by any means. Can we talk?"

"Sure, why not come in? By the way, this is my fiancée, Stephanie." Stephanie smiled at Toby and he nodded back by way of greeting. "Was it anything... urgent?"

Toby slammed the car doors shut. "No, not at all, I just need to ask you a couple of questions. Thought I'd get them out of the way before things start to get busier."

Julian led him into the living room and all three sat down on the sofa, with Julian (rather appropriately, he thought) in the middle. "Okay Toby, over to you."

"Why don't I start with the good news? Things have just picked up on the career front. I could be looking at a promotion, who knows?"

"Well done."

"I'll tell you why. Listen – you remember Stein, don't you? Richard Stein. We met outside his house about a week ago."

Stephanie looked excited. "Yes, that rich guy. He almost became Julian's client. Yes, that – would've been great. So, what about him?"

"Well he was found dead. Murdered in his own home."

"I see," said Julian. "Do you think–"

"What?" Stephanie and Toby asked simultaneously.

"Do you think it was gangland related?"

"Gangland?" Stephanie scowled at Julian.

"We don't know for sure. Organised crime tends to be a couple of bullets. This killing was pretty amateurish. Whack over the head with a heavy object."

"What's this about organised crime?" asked Stephanie.

"That sort of explains my pending promotion. I'd been keeping an eye on Stein for ages, much to the annoyance of my superintendent. Most people had him down as a respectable local businessman, and to all appearances he was. But as I told Julian, that wasn't the real story. He was a drug lord, probably violent."

"You never told me any of this." Stephanie glared at Julian.

"And now that he's dead, I've been put in charge of the case. I know, it's an ill wind and all that."

Stephanie grabbed Julian's knee and squeezed. "Best be thankful. You came so close to taking his money. Lucky escape, I'll say."

Julian nodded slowly. "That's pretty shocking news, Toby. But, when you think about it, is it all that surprising? If you live by the sword, you know?"

Toby shrugged. "Well I suppose he had a pretty good run. He was sixty-two."

"Right," said Julian, "was that all you wanted to tell us?"

"Not quite. There's just one question I need to ask you, if that's okay?"

"Go ahead."

"Where were you at approximately midday on Wednesday the twenty-second of June?"

Julian coughed. "I... I was meeting a friend for a drink. A pint of real ale. His name is Rob. Rob Jollison."

"Great. I assume it'll be no problem for me to contact him and confirm that?"

Julian looked at the floor. "There is a problem. Before we got to the pub he was involved in an accident."

"What sort of accident?"

"He was knocked down by a car."

"So he's in hospital?"

"Yes. In a coma," said Julian. Stephanie gasped. "I went to see him earlier today."

"Sounds terrible," said Toby. "Sorry to hear that. Where did the accident take place?"

"We were crossing North Hill Road, about a hundred yards up from the turning onto Hogarth Road."

"Okay. So you were definitely in the area." Toby jotted something down in a battered leather covered notepad. "Don't worry, it doesn't mean anything at this stage."

Julian opened his wallet and pulled out Mr Syed's business card. "Toby, look, here are the driver's details. If you need to confirm where I was it'd be best to speak to him."

"Sure, thanks Julian. Look, I know all this is overkill, but I'd like to cross you off as soon as possible. It's just that for procedural reasons we need to question everyone who we know has been in contact with Stein. I've met some – *interesting*, shall we say – characters so far."

Julian walked Toby to the front door. Stephanie bit her lip. "So, four hangovers and a near death? Quite a week, I'll say," she muttered.

"Toby, once again, congratulations on your pending promotion. I suppose that will entail a pay rise?" said Julian.

"Yes, hopefully, but I'm not holding out for too much."

"Well every little helps." Julian loathed the ungrammatical cuteness of that expression, but thought it might be appropriate in this case. "You could be saving more, right?"

"Let's see. I will try, though."

"Good. You are – you're still thinking of investing with me, aren't you?"

"You know, I'd almost forgotten. That is something I really want to get round to doing. Ah, I get your point. Yes, I'm going to be saving up extra hard."

"Glad to hear it, Toby."

Toby had opened the front door and was about to leave. "But Julian, just one more thing. I think you know quite a lot about people. In general, I mean – you're good at reading people. What sort of person do you think killed Richard Stein?"

"Someone pretty desperate, that's what I'd say."

"Desperate? In what way?"

"Financially desperate. I think whoever it was wanted to steal from Stein. Either extortion or outright burglary."

"That's highly likely." Toby took a good look around Julian's house: the polished dark wood floors, the white and claret colour scheme, the general sense of space in no hurry to be filled. The owner clearly didn't want for money. "Well, that's my work cut out. I've got to find someone totally strapped for cash who happened to be in the vicinity of Hogarth Road around midday last Wednesday."

"Rob."

"Sorry, who?"

"Robbery. That's the key. Whoever it was, he was intending to rob."

Toby nodded thoughtfully and raised a valedictory salute. Julian walked slowly back into the living room. Stephanie was sitting on the sofa, staring intently at nothing in particular. Julian clasped her hand and pulled it, attempting to lead her upstairs, but she snatched it back. She stared at him. There was more than a hint of a sneer on her fair face. "Just the usual. *Indeed.*"

Chapter 10

Julian leaned back in his chair, almost rocking backwards, and held the edge of the dining table with both hands. The tablecloth was pale yellow with a pretty spring flower pattern. He had eaten a good lunch and was on the verge of needing his afternoon nap, that basic luxury denied to anyone working in an office with a boss breathing down his neck. But this time he thought he'd stay awake for a while longer. It's always polite to thank your host for the meal and attempt interesting conversation. Furthermore, there were some happy thoughts dancing around in his head and he wanted to enjoy them.

He had dealt with things superbly. Stein, Rob, Stephanie and especially Toby had all been handled with just the right touch. Maybe he had a talent for this sort of thing? He felt exhilarated, as if he had – in the words of Winston Churchill, one of his heroes – been shot at without result. He thought of another idol of his, the philosopher Nietzsche, and his concept of the perpetually recurring life. If you were forced to live this life over and over again for all eternity, how would you fill it? Steady state happiness would be a curse, a recipe for eternal boredom. No, you would need the constant variety of pain and pleasure, angst, conflict and victory, frustration and love, mistakes made, people hurt and problems solved; seduction, orgasm, violence. Each incarnation would be a new thrill built upon your previous lives. Julian's recent experiences fitted the bill perfectly. But, for the string of eternal recurrences to work for him, that not-quite-dead-yet manipulator in the heavens would need to furnish him with a more reliable respiratory system.

"Lost in thought again, Jonathan," said his mother. "Some things never change."

"And some things do, mummy. It's Julian now, not Jonathan."

"When you were little you'd often end up talking to yourself after a few minutes away with the fairies. I bet you still do."

"Thanks again for lunch. It was delicious. I'm very glad you still cook now and then." Julian had enjoyed two large helpings of *shakshouka*, the tasty and quick to prepare Moroccan Jewish dish of eggs cracked open into a bubbling pan of spicy tomato and pepper sauce (with lots of onion and garlic, too). It was his mother's staple whenever hungry visitors dropped in for a visit, as the collection of tins of chopped tomato in her cupboard attested.

"I haven't seen you enjoy my cooking for ages. You're used to fancier fare now, aren't you?"

"Nothing I like more than this." Which was the truth – the last few drops of eggy, peppery, tomato sauce had been thoroughly mopped up with rather a lot of pitta bread. Julian looked down at his abdomen. Was there the tiniest hint of an incipient tummy?

"Don't worry. You're not getting fat."

"That's something I'd never ask you about. It would be impossible to get an objective opinion. You remember me as a chubby kid."

"Ah yes, you were so healthy looking back then. Look at you now. Gaunt, grey, thin." Julian rolled his eyes. "Stephanie's starting up a restaurant, isn't that right?"

"Yes, mummy. That's still going ahead."

"Such a lovely girl. You know, I never thought she was serious about you. Well, not at first, anyway."

"Why not?" Julian frowned slightly.

"Well let's face it, you're two very different types of people."

"That can often be a strength. I help her and she helps me."

"Yes, but she's so... well, English, no?"

"I'm English too. What's your point?"

Julian's mother sighed. "Yes, I suppose we are English, in our own way. But Stephanie's posh."

"Ha, yes, I'll give you that. But I'm self-made."

"If you say so."

Julian stared at her. "Most people think I've done pretty well. Taken charge of my career, built a business. Somehow you've never seemed willing to give me any credit."

"No, Julian, that's not true. I'm very happy for you. It's just that–"

"What?" Julian always tried hard not to lose patience with his mother.

"How stable is it? I don't really understand what you're doing. It just seems really risky to go from a steady, well paid job to taking other people's money and making promises."

"Risk scares you, doesn't it, mummy?"

"All our lives your father and I had proper jobs."

"Your idea of a proper job is my idea of boredom and slavery."

"You've always thought that way. You were difficult as a child, too. God knows how you behaved at work when you had a job." She fixed her eyes on him. "A boss can tell if you don't respect his authority, however well you think you can act."

"Anyway, let's get back to Stephanie for a bit, shall we? Her restaurant is expected to be up and running in about six weeks."

"Give her my congratulations. She's a talented girl."

"You should be congratulating me, too. I'm backing her."

"Well, that's what I thought."

"Of course. It's natural for a man to back his future wife. Especially if–"

"He's so successful?" Julian shrugged a long, slow, deliberate shrug. He could not win and frankly, after such a heavy lunch, didn't care to. "One thing, Julian. Stephanie's a very nice girl. Best not to take any risks in that regard." Julian widened his eyes. "I think you understand what I'm saying."

"I just realised something, mummy. You never asked to invest in my fund, did you?"

"No, I'm not interested in any kind of investment. I prefer to keep my money in the bank. At least it's safe." Her expression changed to one of puzzlement, then suspicion. "Julian, do you need me to give you money? Are you in trouble?"

"No, nothing like that! I was just curious about you, that's all. Typical cautious old lady, I suppose."

His mother had wandered into the dining room somewhat absent-mindedly. She was only wearing one of her slippers, the other having been discarded on its side somewhere in the kitchen. Julian thought of Sonia and her red stiletto shoe, casually slipped off that night after a frenzy of dancing. Sonia and his mother were two women at opposite extremes of the same scale. Of course, he needed them both. He visualised lining up four or five Sonias, placed front to back, in order to equal his mother's depth and smiled to himself.

He looked around the dining room of his mother's terraced Edwardian house. The décor was pretty with a vengeance, the flower theme having been repeated in many different sizes, colours and formats. It was as if an interior decorator had been given a sizeable budget and a single instruction: suburban housewife in her late middle years. But Julian didn't care. He actually relished its embarrassing familiarity, its sheer promise of comfort. It represented a sort of ground zero, a base level from which all his other achievements sprang. If everything were to fall apart – true, that was looking less likely now, but who really knew? – he could come back here. Humiliating, yes, but if you weren't trying to impress anyone (how sick he was of that!) and didn't mind some occasional well intentioned nagging you could simply succumb and let this place envelope you in kindness. There really wasn't much of that left anywhere.

Julian looked at his watch. Two o'clock. He probably did have time for a very quick postprandial nap on his mother's couch, but he'd have to set his alarm. Other than food, there was another reason why he had travelled up to her neighbourhood. He had an important speaking engagement to attend. At three thirty precisely he would be addressing a large group of seventeen and eighteen year olds, A-level students at his old school. His reputation had, ultimately, spread a little further than he would have preferred and the headmaster of his alma mater – a Mr Geoffrey Standing – had invited him to speak to the pupils. Everyone wanted to 'work in finance' these days. Julian himself never had, but since his arm had been twisted into providing them with advice and motivation – "our students are always hugely encouraged by old boys and girls who have, shall we say, 'made it'" – he thought the best he could do would be to make an appearance and give a speech based on the career of some imaginary, perfect City banker, one who would expertly invest in weapons manufacturers but never be so foolish as to actually get blood on his own hands.

St Jude's Church of England school consisted of one fine old building housing the headmaster's and administrative offices, where Julian was supposed to report, and a large array of temporary looking, wooden, chipboard or plastic structures forming the classrooms, workshops and science laboratories. These facilities had expanded vastly since he had been there. He entered the old building and inhaled. Yes, it smelled the same (clearly schools had not made the same effort that hospitals had) and it was as if he were a pupil there once more. He half expected some sloppy oaf to make fun of his haircut, then ask for help with his maths assignment later that same day.

"Welcome back to St Jude's, Julian!" Mr Standing shook his hand heartily and told him it would be best to start the talk as soon as possible. "You're bang on time, and the students are already seated and waiting. If you have a few minutes afterwards, you and I should talk."

Julian looked at the array of eager expressions and straight postures. "Right, hello everyone. My name's Julian Kay and I've been asked by Mr Standing to say a few words about working in finance. Young, intelligent people like you have a lot of choices, and I'm sure at least some of you have thought seriously about a career in banking or the financial markets." Many of them nodded. They looked serious, business like, ready to pounce on any titbit of information that would give them an edge in that desperate battle to be interviewed and hired, to be allowed entry to the circle of prestige and untold prosperity. Julian had the facts well rehearsed and was, obviously, very good at sounding like he knew what he was talking about. The words flowed as he studied the faces of the young people in front of him.

How beautiful they all looked! Fresh, keen and innocent – that's what Julian was (approximately; who counts, anyway?) twenty years ago. He almost wanted to be sitting among them, getting to know them on a more personal level. He caught sight of a particularly chiselled young lady: the lightest natural tan, a delicate nose and chin, scraped back dark hair and sharply contrasting blue eyes peering from behind thick black glasses. A redhead with her hair in decorative tight braids took notes furiously, the tip of her tongue making intermittent appearances at the corner of her mouth. A slightly plump but pretty blonde with several shirt buttons undone sat back, half smiling, really just happy to be doing nothing and because the school day was almost over. Her friend, a slender, junior Cleopatra complete with glossy black hair and skin that you could believe had been bathed in ass's milk struggled to stay awake (why so sleep deprived?) High summer, of course, had had its predictable fashion impact: there was a preponderance of bare calves, some slender, others bordering on the athletic; short socks or none at all, but plenty of ankle bracelets (what a trend!) glittering in the sunlight that streamed in obliquely through the window. Feet waited patiently inside strappy sandals, dangled a shoe from the big toe or merely rested nakedly on top of ballet pumps for the sheer cooling comfort that provided. Finely turned ankles and smooth knees tapped, full, pink lips pouted, chests heaved and long, beautifully manicured fingernails wandered inside perfectly bleached blouses or up shockingly abbreviated skirts for a well-deserved late afternoon scratch. But nowhere – and Julian had surveyed the crowd several times to make sure – nowhere did he see a budding Sonia, a petite, dark eyed intellectual with no use for the conventional world of work or careers.

His speech had come to an end. He nodded at Mr Standing who had been sitting in the corner. "Any questions?" he asked the audience, trying to make contact with the pretty blue eyes behind the glasses.

A lanky young man with acne, messy hair and an overactive Adam's apple raised his hand. "Yes?" said Julian.

The questioner cleared his throat. "What would you say was the most important personal quality required for a successful career in finance?" It was the deepest voice Julian had ever heard from so pencil-like a chest.

"Integrity. Without your own unshakeable personal standards, your own moral code, you are unlikely to survive long in this business." The young audience seemed to like that answer. They began to clap, and Julian realised some of the girls in the front row were smiling sweetly at him. As the crowd dispersed, he said in a quieter voice, "If some of you would like to talk in more detail, I'll be here at the front for a while longer."

Most of the students were in a hurry to go home but the lazy blonde and Cleopatra made their way to the front. Julian had thought they'd be the ones least likely to show any interest. They walked right up to him so that they were standing very close. They looked at each other, giggled a little and then looked at him. "Hi," they said.

"Hello. Hope you found my talk useful. What can I do for you?"

"Just wanted to ask you a few questions about your... career." They looked at each other again, then the Egyptian princess spoke. "How long have you been doing this?"

Julian exhaled through rounded lips and looked at the ceiling. "A long time. Most of my career. Let's say at least ten years."

"So you're still quite young, then?" The blonde's plump lips were glossy.

"That really depends on what you mean by young, I suppose."

"People in finance earn – they're very well remunerated, aren't they?" she enquired.

"They can be. It depends on so many things."

"Can I ask you something?" said the beauty of the Nile, "what sort of car do you drive?" The blonde looked at her viciously and rolled her eyes. "Sorry, I mean–"

"Nothing particularly flash. It's not really like that, you know."

The two girls started to get nervous and looked at the floor. Julian smiled and put the fingertips of both hands together. It was the dark one who spoke. "Could you give us your contact details, please?"

"Of course." He pulled out a business card and gave it to the blonde.

"Thank you," they said, simultaneously and very endearingly before walking off. There were times when Julian felt he would make a very good father.

Afterwards, in Mr Standing's study, Julian drank a cup of coffee and gracefully accepted the headmaster's praise. "Thank you, Julian. They really enjoyed that. Gave them plenty to think about, too." He sighed. "That's really what society lacks these days."

"What's that? What does society lack?"

"Mentors. Those who can point the way ahead for younger people, show them the correct path. Invaluable. Almost as important – no, every bit as important – as good teachers. Those kids were transfixed."

"Yes. You're absolutely right about mentoring. I hadn't really thought about it."

"Julian, before you go – I know you're not one to toot your own horn, but I have heard quite a lot about how well you've been doing. You know, with the investment fund."

"Oh. Okay. Thank you." Julian could sense what was coming next.

"I am seriously impressed. Compared to the interest you can get from a bank account – which, let's face it, is lacklustre at the best of times! – you seem to have squared the circle. Something in the region of thirty percent per year without risk, as I understand? That's truly remarkable."

Julian nodded and gave the headmaster a tight smile. "Thank you."

"You know, Julian, I've always made fundraising a priority at St Jude's. Take our swimming pool, for example. It's not been very long since we've actually had one. Now, of course, we need to make improvements. I won't go as far as saying we need an Olympic sized pool – ha, no, not yet – but a professional quality competition pool – I mean, why not? We have some keen, some very good up and coming swimming talent. They deserve no less. By the way" – he smiled warmly at Julian – "what was your sport when you were a pupil here?"

Julian had always avoided sports as far as possible, forging sick notes whenever the need had arisen. "Actually, I was on the debating team."

"Aha, right. Well, still a team player. Anyway, as I was saying, our little fund has been accumulating and, I'm rather pleased to tell you, has now grown to quite a healthy sum. Approaching six figures. What we could really do with right now is a substantial boost to our investment returns, something that could, sooner rather than later – if you know what I mean – get us to the stage where mere desire becomes financial reality. That's when we could really take our facilities here at St Jude's to the next level. Do the kids proud. What, if you don't mind me asking, is your minimum investment?"

Julian had prepared a response. "You know, I'd love to be able to help. The problem is, I can't accept money from charitable or educational organisations. Regulations, you see."

"Right. Why is that, exactly?"

"Don't ask me," Julian shrugged, "there's so much red tape involved. The rules change all the time. The best I can do is try to keep up. Government, eh? Who needs it? All their interfering."

"Red tape. I know." The headmaster sat very still with one hand supporting his chin. He was doing a pretty good job of hiding his frustration. Julian noticed he had about ten long hairs which started from his forehead and had been combed back all the way to the nape of his neck, traversing an otherwise featureless bald head. All ten were quivering.

"Sorry about that, Mr Standing," said Julian. But he wasn't sorry. He had retired from the business and that was that. He got up to leave. He had a spare couple of hours before he had to go home for a dinner cooked by Stephanie – her mood had improved and she'd agreed to let him assess some of her new restaurant dishes. Yes, he would pop back to his mother's, have his well deserved nap and ask her to pack up the remnants of lunch (there had been quite a bit left over) for him to take home.

He reflected on his day so far. He had visited his mother, the way a dutiful son should, and helped some young people find their direction in life. Two good deeds in a single afternoon.

Chapter 11

Julian had thought he would eat only very lightly at dinner – having to force himself to sample a mouthful from the range of smallish dishes Stephanie had prepared – but in fact ended up polishing off almost everything on the table. From the look on her face she took this as a compliment. He also sensed some sort of mild relief from her. A husband with the beginnings of a pot belly was always a safer bet. Less likely to wander.

Stephanie had expected Julian to nominate a favourite recipe, one that he wouldn't mind being named after him, but he told her he would need to try her full range before making a decision. She looked exhausted. Julian too thought he would simply begin to doze off after eating so well, but actually felt very alert for this time of the evening (no doubt the nap had helped). He was ready for something exciting to happen, one last frisson of risk before turning in for the night. Sonia? After Stephanie had climbed to the top of the stairs he pulled out his phone. A message was waiting for him. Sonia had texted him at 15:44, while he had been talking to the pupils.

"Julian, how are you? Can we meet? Sonia X"

He sent her one back: "Hi, yes, I was just thinking of you. What time?"

"Oh great, how about half an hour from now, the usual meeting point?"

"Agreed," Julian typed.

"Also, PLEASE I don't like to ask but can you bring money? Things are *very* tight here XX"

"Ok." Julian had expected something along those lines.

"Oh thank you SO much. Please, whatever you can manage XXX"

Julian was dressed semi formally and couldn't be bothered to change (not that there was any particular need to.) He had been to the cashpoint that morning and hadn't spent much. He would give Sonia whatever was left in his wallet. No doubt her casino jackpot had disappeared in roughly the same amount of time it had taken her to win it.

The walk up to the winding high street felt different. Each footfall was light and he sensed no need to look over his shoulder. The feeling of freedom was odd, as if there were too much of it, along with a surfeit of space and a summer evening that required not the slightest adjustment to his clothes.

The two of them were waiting for him, the girl and her chaperone. The burly companion (wearing his lightest summer raincoat) waved to Julian as soon as he entered their range of vision. A whole new era of trust – friendship, almost – seemed to have developed. Julian received a firm clasp and a squeeze on the shoulder and something approaching a smile. Raincoat Man nodded once to Sonia and walked off.

Julian bent down and Sonia brushed her dry lips against his. "We may as well have coffee," he said, "assuming you've already had dinner?"

"I did have something to eat," said Sonia, "so coffee will be fine. I'll probably have some cake, too. I'm still a little hungry."

Julian looked at the girl he had bowed his head to kiss: no high heels. In fact, no attempt at glamour whatsoever – this was the student he had first met. She was wearing the flat black sandals she'd had on that day when he had tried to read over her shoulder. His mouth made a small smile and she caught his eye, giving him a hint of one back. They entered Café Franz and sat down in the corner.

A waitress (the one who usually took forever to attend to Julian) immediately walked over to Sonia and took her order. "I'll have a large café latte please – can you use that oversized china mug? – and two almond croissants. And maybe a pain au chocolate. Thanks!" Julian quickly mentioned that he wanted a small white coffee before the waitress strode off.

Sonia widened her eyes and looked hard at Julian. She looked down and then back up at him from under her fringe. The front teeth began to bite the plump lower lip... ah yes, of course. Julian got his wallet out and gave her all the notes he had, something like a hundred and fifty pounds. There was no one sitting near them to notice. "Thank you, Julian," she said. Without looking at it she slipped the money somewhere inside her black halter top.

"Sonia, how did that Dostoyevsky essay go in the end? What mark did you get?" He realised that, curiously, he was taking a deep interest in her education and progress.

"I got a 'B'"

Only a 'B'? Julian frowned. "What was the subject?"

"Can a moral system be absolute or only ever relative? Discuss."

"Well that should have given you quite a bit to write about," said Julian, smiling.

"What answer would you have given?"

"You know what, Sonia? You can only ever be honest and answer a question like that from your own perspective."

"So tell me what would you have written."

"Well, anyone who lives in the real world has to make choices. Most people have to choose between two or more undesirable alternatives. So picking the least bad option is the closest we can get to true morality."

"When you say 'bad', whose perspective is that from?"

"I mean good or bad from society's point of view. Essentially what helps or harms the greatest number of people."

"And you actually believe that? What about if you want something different from what society does? Something other people don't want you to have. Can't you have your own moral code?"

Julian frowned again and cleared his throat. "You know Sonia, you should be getting better grades than a 'B'. A clever girl like you should be acing it."

"Yes, I know."

"So, what's the problem?"

"I just don't have enough time to study. I have to earn cash. Somehow."

"Yes, I understand. You said the situation was very tight money wise. What's going on?"

She shrugged a long, slow "don't know" and for the first time looked truly perplexed. "Those evening jobs I used to do. You know, the dinners, the entertaining. They've all suddenly dried up. Nothing. Zilch." The waitress came back to their table with the coffees and Sonia's patisserie feast. She slurped the latte and took a large bite out of one of one of the croissants. The enthusiastic chewing that followed seemed to raise her spirits momentarily.

"You know what? I think there's going to be an economic downturn. People will be spending much less money from now on."

She nodded slowly while eating as quickly as possible. "Yes, maybe that's the reason." Another large gulp of milky coffee followed. "It's weird, though, how I've heard nothing whatsoever from the boss. It's all gone dead quiet."

"So," ventured Julian, "you should have more time to study at night?"

Sonia shook her head briskly and spoke with her mouth full: "No. Actually, I've just started doing something else in the evenings. I'm in training at the moment but it should end up being quite lucrative."

"What's this new job then?"

"I'll tell you later. But Julian," – she pointed the coffee spoon at him and stabbed the air a couple of times – "there's something I really need to ask you about."

"Go ahead."

"Have you seen Rob recently?"

Julian's stomach lurched. He tried to keep calm. "Uh? Oh Rob, yes. Why do you ask?"

"He seems to have gone silent."

"Silent? As in not returning your calls?"

That puzzled look – the wide eyes emphasising the smallness of the other features – returned to her face. It made her look even younger than the student garb she had reverted to. "Well, yes. I suppose that's what I mean."

"Did you two have a bit of a falling out?" Julian made his concerned face.

"No. Not at all."

"You actually get along rather well, don't you?"

"Look, we had arranged to meet. In a bookshop, funnily enough. The one next to here."

"And what happened?"

"He didn't show up. Strange. He'd seemed so keen to meet me."

"Sonia, I've got to tell you something. Rob was involved in a traffic accident."

"When? You could have told me earlier!"

"Sorry. Look, it happened last Wednesday. He got knocked down by a car. He's in hospital right now."

"Hospital? Is he okay?"

"He's at the Royal Northwest." Julian pointed towards the street and indicated downhill. "He's unconscious – in a coma, actually. Sorry to have to tell you this."

Sonia gasped silently and held a hand over her mouth. "Thanks for letting me know. I'm going to visit him first thing tomorrow."

"It's family only at the moment."

She shrugged. "I'll find a way in. Julian – were you with him at the time?"

"No. I was at home, working. His mother contacted me and told me as I'm his nearest close friend." He put his hand on Sonia's clenched fist. "I can see you're upset."

"No – well, yes, I'm a bit shocked." She shook slightly and wiped something from her eye. "Sorry. It's nothing."

"You like Rob, don't you?"

"Back to your favourite subject, I see." She smiled wearily. "Actually, yes, I do." Julian nodded; yes, he had thought so. "But not in the way you think. For a man – I mean, the man in my life – I need..." She looked up and to the side, temporarily lost, it seemed to Julian, in some ideal world in which exemplary men always did what their women wanted without being asked.

"What?" he prodded.

"Basically a man I can rely on. Someone who can support me. When all that initial fuss is over with – you know, dating, kissing, sex, all that stuff – what is there?"

"You forgot arguing. What's left? Well – a relationship?"

"Yeah sure, but what does that mean?"

Julian tried to look as if he were thinking deeply. "Trust. That's probably what holds things together, ultimately." He stifled a cough.

"I used to think that. It's just that the men I trust are not usually the ones I'm... I'm attracted to."

"Interesting. You like to make life difficult for yourself."

"I've always gone for older men." Julian kept himself calm and tried not to look excited. "Mature, who've really lived and established their lives. Wives, children depending on them. Plus, you never really know if you've got them or not. You've always got that uncertainty. I find that really sexy."

"I understand you."

"You know, you are rather attractive. For an older guy." Sonia made a gesture – Julian wasn't quite sure what exactly she had done; was it a slight flick of her hair? An imperceptible raising of her eyebrows? – and the waitress who disliked him came rushing over to their table. "The bill, please," said Sonia. Julian pulled his wallet out as the waitress ran off to tot up what they had ordered.

Sonia matched his wallet with an embossed business card, extracted from somewhere inside that halter top (not the same place she had stashed the money.) She handed it to him. "I've got to go now, but come and see me at this place during the week." She rubbed his knuckles softly with two fingertips.

Julian held the card at arm's length and looked at it. *PROMISES – the newest and hottest gentlemen's club to open in the West End this year. This card enables a group of five or more to enter free of charge. Normal entry £15.* "Your new job?" he asked. Sonia smiled and nodded.

They stood outside the entrance to Café Franz. She wrapped her bare arms around his neck and stood as tall as she could on the tips of her toes (there were no heels this time to provide any assistance with her height). She pressed her open mouth against his, forcefully, and inserted her tongue. She caressed his hungrily. Julian tasted almonds, coffee, chocolate and college girl so intensely that he was tempted to close his eyes (something he never did while kissing) to block out any other sensation. Sonia had another trick up her sleeve. Small, slender fingers began to play with his lower shirt buttons as the kissing progressed. They quickly gave up on the intricate task of undoing them and made their way to the top of his waistband and hovered, dancing uncertainly like a butterfly's legs. Julian shifted his position so they weren't standing directly in front of the main door. The fingers slid downwards. "Ooh, some chub. I like a bit of a tummy on a man." Down they went and then they were in their element. They tickled, squeezed and pulled, alternating between tender, delicate stroking and some dark, wild battle they had almost been designed to fight. One minute later a sharp, stinging flick of a fingernail signalled the end had come (for the time being).

Julian began to limp but quickly resolved to walk home normally as if nothing had happened (in fact, nothing *had* happened). "Don't forget about that card I gave you," Sonia called back to him. "Come and see me. I'm there week nights only, Monday to Thursday."

Julian opened the front door, took off his shoes and padded up the stairs silently. He pushed open the bedroom door as slowly as it would move. Stephanie was asleep, half curled up on her side under the single sheet. She must have collapsed into that position. Julian undressed and got into bed wearing his boxer shorts only – a level of nudity he considered optimal: not too suggestive, yet leaving the door open to a range of further developments. He lay on his back and put his hands behind his head.

Breathing softly, he wondered if his pounding heartbeat would be amplified by the tautness of the oversized mattress and the emptiness of the cavernous bedchamber. Had Stephanie heard him? He was lying perfectly still and watching her. Her breathing was light, so shallow that no part of her moved. At that instant some image or storyline in whatever dream she was having caused her to spring up onto her knees in the manner of an oversized, lanky white cat. She was completely naked. Half awake, half grinning, she knee-walked towards Julian and climbed astride him, making sure to pin him down totally with her shins on his shoulders, her knees positioned next to his ears. There was no hope of escape. Julian looked up at the gentle curve of her belly and the near spherical breasts with their barely discernible nipples.

"I've never worked out what you do," she yawned, "in the time between me falling asleep and you managing to get up here. It'll remain a mystery." She rested her palms on his chest and pressed downward. "But you smell very nice. Like honey. And... something else. Not sure what, but I like it." She started gently rubbing and tickling different areas of his chest. She pinched a clump of hairs and playfully tugged.

Her talented thumbs, with their perfectly buffed long nails, coupled with Sonia's deft fingerwork earlier made Julian forget all about the day's overeating and that bloated feeling in his stomach. He decided not to go to sleep just yet.

Chapter 12

Julian firmly believed that favours should be paid back in full, and ideally as promptly as possible. Stephanie's culinary and sensual dispensations were no exception and, early the following morning, he found himself chopping up carrots and onions in the newly built kitchen in the high street premises of her restaurant (it was due to open in a couple of weeks). True, he was slow and clumsy, but he knew it was his good intentions that mattered. Furthermore, he needed to be extra careful to make sure he didn't cut himself (that chef's knife of hers looked lethal). All in all, apart from the fact it was taking him three times as long as normal to dice carrots, the effort was worth it. His cubes had a degree of refinement and character, he thought, that an average sous chef could only dream of.

"How are you getting along, darling?" Stephanie had poked her head around the redbrick divide that partially sectioned off the kitchen from the main dining area. "I can see you're being very careful with that knife. Just as well, to be honest. We all remember what happened the last time we let you loose with one." Julian rubbed his left index finger and shivered.

Allegra was standing next to Stephanie. "I think he's doing really well. What sweet little carrot cubes!"

"Tell me, Stephanie and Allegra," said Julian, "when this place is finished – fully up and running – what's it going to be called?"

"I had a suggestion," said Allegra. "The Lotus Goddess. Stephanie is still mulling it over."

"That's not a bad name, actually," said Stephanie. "Let me think about it. I won't ask whom you had in mind, Allegra, when you thought of a goddess."

Julian had assumed the duration of this favour returning would be entirely up to him, that he'd be able to simply walk off as soon as he felt bored. For some reason, he wasn't; the careful carrot positioning and cutting seemed to have some sort of calming, therapeutic effect on him. It fitted his definition of 'useful work' – maybe that was it? It was a chance to contribute to the activity of real people in the physical world.

As he continued to chop the cubes became neater and more uniform and their rate of production increased. Practice – yes, soon he would be a pro. He realised his main career had now come to an end. He would need something to occupy himself with. How about being his future wife's devoted kitchen assistant? Or better still, restaurant manager? The rock, the indispensable go to man for a rising star chef. He sighed. It was a decent reserve plan, if nothing else. Apart from the fact he couldn't actually imagine himself working for his wife. Investor, yes, employee – no, that would never work.

He realised what the kitchen work was doing: making him more human. He was just an empty shell now, one with a vacuum of amorality inside. He had wanted to break down, collapse and cry; to tell someone – anyone. He gripped the knife handle so hard that it became painful... and the bad feelings subsided.

Just at that moment he heard some familiar footsteps, brisk and heavy. The still whitewashed glass door of the restaurant swung open and Toby walked in. He was perspiring and out of breath.

Julian put the knife down and looked up. He tried to smile. "Toby! What a nice surprise. I didn't hear your Porsche engine. Did you have to park a few streets away? This area has crazy restrictions."

Smiling, Toby walked up to Julian. "Hello Julian." He pointed at his carrot cubes. "Quite the chef, I see!"

"Yes, well, it's good to have a second string to one's bow. How did you know I'd be here?"

"Well I actually called round at your house initially. There was no one in. Then I realised you both must be at work." Stephanie had entered the main dining area and smiled at Toby. Allegra looked on.

"Yes, well, I wouldn't call this work as such. I'm just helping Steph. How–"

"Right, yes, I got talking to that neighbour of yours, George... Crumb, is it? He told me that you'd – that Stephanie had just started a restaurant up on the high street and that I should try my luck there."

George McCrum had always had a soft spot for Stephanie and had often enjoyed long conversations with her. She didn't seem to mind the attention in the slightest. Julian managed a tight smile. "George, yes. He usually knows what's going on."

"Interesting chap. Very intelligent from what I gathered. We were having a chat about you, in fact. He used to be a customer of your investment fund, right?"

"Yes, that's right. I think he did pretty well out of it."

"But for some reason he decided to cash in and withdraw everything. He didn't tell me why."

"George cancelled? Really?" said Stephanie.

"You know what, Toby? Some people lose their nerve. We've been producing exceptional returns – risk free returns – for years now. I suppose he just got cold feet and thought it couldn't go on."

Toby shrugged. "Yes I see. Seems like a shame. Anyway he was useful enough to let me know where you were. So I walked all the way up the hill. Pretty good exercise!"

"Walked? Why? Is your car being repaired?"

"Ah," smiled Toby, "I haven't told you the good news. The Porsche is on the market. I've assigned it back to the dealership to sell it for me. With a bit of luck I should be able to raise twenty-five grand, even after their commission is taken into account."

"Good news? Why are you selling it, Toby? I thought you loved that car."

"So I can invest with you, Julian. I've always said I would and now I've found a way. I don't know why I didn't think of it earlier. Heather's got a list as long as my arm of stuff we need to buy for the flat. Not to mention that she hasn't been on any week end spa breaks for a year."

So it had finally happened – at exactly the wrong time. Julian tried to look happy. "That's excellent news, Toby. How – uh, long do you think it will take to sell your car?"

"In this market, not long. Things may have slowed down a tiny bit but it's still looking healthy."

"About a month, d'you reckon?" Toby nodded, clearly considering that a pretty good estimate. Right. So Julian had a month or so to keep Toby excited and on his side. Enough time to get himself out of the frame – after which he could let Toby down gently. "So, any luck with the case? Stein, I mean."

"Yes, actually. There are one or two points I need to clarify with you – no big deal, don't worry – but other than that it looks like progress is being made. I might even be on the verge of that promotion. Fingers crossed, but a pay rise on top of your investment magic would be a godsend."

"Indeed it would. Good luck."

"So, the one thing I wanted to clarify – just to get this out of the way once and for all – is why you were with Rob at the time he had the accident. What was the purpose of your meeting?"

Julian swallowed hard, causing Toby to frown. "I think I told you. Didn't I? We were meeting up for a drink."

"Yes, you did tell me that." Toby looked around the restaurant, his eyes finally settling on Stephanie and Allegra who were supposedly hard at work on some supplier accounts. But it was clear to both him and Julian that the women's ears were burning. Toby lowered his voice a notch. "Julian, I had a chat with Mr Syed. He told me you were dressed for a business meeting. Apparently you had your briefcase with you. Is that right?"

"What else did Mr Syed say?"

"Not a lot. Just that he had never seen anyone behave as strangely as Rob that day. It was as if his legs had a mind of their own, the way he just jumped into the road like that."

Julian nodded. "Yes, he did seem to be in a pretty strange mood that day." How much would Rob remember when he woke up? Julian felt his heart beat harder and faster.

"So—"

"Yes, why did I have my briefcase with me. Well..." – Julian thought quickly – "I had been planning on visiting a client after our drink—"

"Can you tell me which one?"

He swallowed again. "But... actually decided against it at the last minute. I thought I might end up having more than just the one pint and not be in a proper state to talk business. I had the briefcase packed already. I just sort of picked it up automatically on my way out of the house."

"Right." Toby looked thoughtful. "What was in the briefcase?"

"Some paperwork. A lot of documentation on the investment fund, in fact. Legal notices, disclaimers, that sort of thing." He smiled at Toby. "You'll have to wade through all that soon, if you decide to come on board."

"Yes, I'm sure. Okay, so back to this drink with Rob. The one that never happened. You bumped into him on North Hill Road, right? Presumably you were both on your way to the pub."

"Yes, that's right. The Railway pub."

"It's just that we've been through all the calls and texts he sent over the previous several days and there was no record of him arranging anything with you."

"Toby, Rob and I are practically neighbours. We only live a ten minute walk apart and bump into each other all the time. We made a verbal agreement to meet. Just a few days before."

"I see. But interestingly, according to the text messages he *had* sent, he was supposed to meet up with someone in Hamble's bookshop, just up here on the high street. Someone known only as 'S' according to his contact list. Any idea who that could be?"

"No idea. He must have had some other engagements planned after our drink." The police could trace names and addresses from phone numbers. Would they bother going down that route? If so, why? After all, Rob hadn't died.

Toby sighed. Was there anything else? He seemed to be racking his brain. "O-kay," he said at last. "I think that's about it. That's all I need to ask you regarding your movements that day."

"Right. Well, I'm glad to have been of assistance. Was there, uh–"

"Actually yes, there was. Julian, I want to find out a bit more about Rob. Some details about his life. How well did you know him?"

It had clearly all become too much for Stephanie. "They're best friends. Inseparable!" she called out. Julian nodded submissively.

"Right, that's going to be useful. For how long have you known him?"

"Since we were at university together. Roughly twenty years."

"Excellent. So you two are very close. I must say, it must be a very worrying time for you right now, no doubt."

"Why?" Julian momentarily felt alarmed. "Oh the accident, my God, yes. It has been a terribly anxious few days."

Toby put his hand on Julian's arm and left it there for a second. "Do you have any idea why he was behaving so absent-mindedly when you met him? Had anything unusual happened to him recently?"

Julian looked blank (an expression he had long ago perfected). "Not that I'm aware of."

Toby continued, "I should tell you one thing. I made some enquiries at his place of residence. He was occupying a room in a shared house, oddly enough on Hobart Road. He was practically Stein's next neighbour."

"Yes, he told me he had moved. I never got round to seeing this new place of his."

"Do you know if he got along with his housemates?"

"I would assume so. Rob was – is very easy to get on with."

"Well," said Toby, "I managed to get a chance to speak to a couple of them. They told me something I had suspected, and which might turn out to be pretty relevant to this case."

"What's that?" Julian was curious.

"They told me he was behind with his rent. Would that be something unusual for Rob?"

"I'm sure Rob would make every effort to pay everything he owed. He's both honest and meticulous."

"So can we assume he was in some sort of financial difficulty?"

"That's probably a fair assumption. He told me they were making people redundant at work. I think he was unlucky and got picked for the chop."

"Aha. Well, things are beginning to fall into place. I believe we're making some progress here," said Toby.

"Okay," said Julian, nodding.

"One more thing," continued Toby, "whenever the two of you would meet up, was alcohol always involved?"

"Yes, and lots of it, too," said Stephanie. The supplier invoices had completely lost her interest. She was sitting up straight and alert, listening to every word of their conversation. "If it weren't for Rob's influence,

243

Julian probably wouldn't touch the stuff. Apart from important social occasions, of course."

Toby looked at Stephanie. "How well do you know Rob?"

"Well, I, you know–"

"She hasn't met him. I never quite got round to introducing them to each other. Please continue, Toby."

"Right. Well the impression I'm forming of Rob is that he had some issues with alcohol. A drink problem, in other words. Would you agree with that, Julian?"

"I'd say he liked a drink or two. Often a few more. But an actual problem? No, not really."

"His housemates had a different view. They told me they'd often smelt drink on his breath – throughout the working week as well as week ends – and noticed some pretty odd behaviour too. Absent mindedness, lack of communication, that sort of thing."

"I suppose there could be times when he wasn't himself. Same with all of us, really. What are you getting at exactly?"

"He seems to be the most likely suspect right now. That's my current theory." Julian widened his eyes.

"You mean you think he killed Mr Stein?" Stephanie put her hand to her open mouth. A second later she removed it. "Maybe it's not all that surprising, the more I think about it."

"Was his behaviour ever aggressive?" asked Toby. "Particularly after drinking."

"No. Rowdy, maybe, sort of over enthusiastic. A bit physical perhaps."

"Julian," he continued, "do you think Rob is capable of violence?"

Julian looked him straight in the eye. "I wouldn't have thought so. But I cannot be one hundred percent sure."

"No, absolutely. You never really know what's going on inside."

Julian steadied himself for one last, big bluff: "Actually, it doesn't happen very often, but... Rob has been known to totally lose it. I've only seen it once or twice. It happens due to stress." He paused. "It's bizarre to see such a laid back person turn so aggressive. It's scary."

"I see," said Toby, very quietly. Everyone fell silent. No one in the room wanted to be the first to speak.

Julian cleared his throat. "So, uh, what do you think happened?"

"Well," said Toby, "there are two things we know for sure. Two things that are facts. Firstly, he was in trouble financially, and secondly, he wasn't always capable of controlling his alcohol intake. There's a third factor too, but that's more opinion than fact."

"What's that?"

"According to the people he was house sharing with his behaviour had been odd. Pretty distant. Ah yes, we do know one more thing – a fact, that is. He knew Mr Stein. He was on conversational terms with him."

"Really?"

"Yes, one girl who lives in the house confirmed that. She had seen them chatting."

"And?"

"This is my theory. Okay, we've got this chap, Rob – a simple fellow, happy go lucky – who is just about surviving financially, making ends meet. Life is good for him, up to a point: he has a job, a roof over his head in a nice area, enough to eat and, more importantly, drink. Then things start to go wrong. His company starts making cuts, letting people go. He goes from flat at the end of the month to being behind with the rent. Relations with his housemates sour. One day it all just gets too much for Rob. Maybe a bad day at work, or someone shoving him on the tube. He's angry and he needs money. He's met Stein a couple of times and knows he's wealthy. And therefore an obvious target. He invites himself in and, well... from there things get out of control."

Julian nodded. "Yes, that makes sense."

"You know, Julian," said Toby, "in my line of work you end up getting to know all sorts of characters and their life stories. It can be fascinating. Nothing is ever as it seems at first. That's probably what keeps me in this gig. For example, the relationship between you and Rob – curious, let's face it. Different personalities, different social strata – but you've been close friends for most of your adult lives. And then one of you, out of the blue, discovers that the person you thought you knew really well is actually someone completely alien. It must feel as if the last twenty years has been completely turned on its head. And to think, you were just trying to fit in an innocent drink between business meetings!" He shook his head slowly, disbelievingly.

"Yes, it's weird how you think you can know people," agreed Julian, "and then all of a sudden watch them change. Or maybe simply reveal what they've always been hiding.

"One good thing may come out of all this," said Stephanie. "Julian won't have such a dedicated drinking partner. One who'll show up anywhere and everywhere booze is on offer."

Toby and Julian looked at her, then at each other. Toby started to chuckle. "In a way it makes me laugh, all this fuss. Over Richard Stein. The man was a criminal. A really unpleasant piece of work, for God's sake." Julian frowned. "This is me being a careerist, I suppose. There are more deserving cases out there, for sure, but Stein is my patch. I'm going to get to the bottom of this. I owe it to myself."

"You might be onto something, Toby. Who knows. I wish I could have been more helpful."

"You've been a lot of help, Julian. Thank you. Seriously." Toby waved, turned around and walked towards the door. Just before leaving he turned back. "Remember Julian, just one more month now. Just a few more weeks and I'm in. A fully fledged investor. Take care, my friend. And be careful about any new clients. Remember – full background checks are a must!"

There was complete silence as soon as Toby had left. There was so much that needed to be discussed that none of the three restaurateurs knew where to start – or dared to speak. They each continued with their task with a grim sense of purpose, total focus. Julian bowed his head, picked up the knife with his right hand and grabbed a couple of large carrots with his left. He knew his cubes would soon be bordering on perfection.

The main door of the restaurant opened again, but this time gingerly. There had been no audible footsteps or voices. A girl walked in. A single, violent heartbeat stabbed Julian in the chest. She was young, smallish and brunette, smartly dressed and wearing high heels. It was Sonia. Julian looked down quickly and studied the interplay of knife edge and carrot flesh in minute detail. At that moment nothing else on earth could have fascinated him more. He slouched and shrivelled, willing himself to disappear by sheer bad posture alone. By swivelling his eyes upwards he could view Sonia up to the bottom of her neck – where the dark brown bob ended – without catching her eye.

Stephanie and Allegra looked up from their invoices. They stared at Sonia, half smiling. "Hello," said Stephanie, "can I help you?"

"Hello, yes, I think you can," said Sonia, walking over to their table. "Is this a restaurant?"

"Yes. Or rather, it will be soon. Give it about three weeks from today."

"I see." Sonia looked around the premises, thoroughly surveying every interior feature. Julian noticed that she had managed to completely avoid looking at him. "I like what you've done here. That open kitchen." She waved a hand in Julian's direction. "Very stylish."

"Thank you," said Stephanie. "Yes, we thought it would look nice and make the most of the space we have here."

"It really does." Sonia looked thoughtful (Julian now and then dared to take flickering glances at her face). "It must be pretty expensive to fit out a restaurant. Quite an undertaking."

"Tell me about it!" said Stephanie. "That's always the biggest outlay. Once you've got that out of the way your day to day running costs are usually manageable." Sonia nodded sagely.

Sonia and Stephanie, the two women in Julian's life, were getting to know each other. Building a rapport. Right here in front of him while he, like some eastern yogic master, willed himself into invisibility (he was pretty sure it was actually happening). Neither had glanced at him so much as once. It was frightening, but thrilling. He felt a shiver of pleasure ripple down his slumped, by now surely crumbling spine.

"Well, we hope to see you here again soon. As one of our first customers," said Allegra.

"What sort of food will you specialise in?" asked Sonia.

"Indian regional cuisine."

"Oh God, I love curry. Once I start eating I just can't stop myself." Stephanie and Allegra looked up and down Sonia's small, thin frame with its tennis ball breasts. They looked at each other, visibly trying not to laugh.

"By the way, I like your shoes," said Allegra, pointing at the red stilettos.

"Thank you. They were a present." Julian's head bowed even lower.

"Well, lucky you."

Stephanie and Allegra looked down at their accounts, reminding themselves where they had got to at the point this curious young woman had walked in. Sonia started walking languorously around the restaurant, talking long, leisurely steps, stretching her slim legs out to their fullest extent. Her high heels made a slow, ominous clicking noise on the new floor tiles, a relentless countdown to some unknowable but inevitable denouement that would, Julian knew, make him regret ever having asked her about that book she'd been reading.

Sonia walked past Julian. They looked at each other and she gave him a brief, expressionless smile, the sort of cursory acknowledgement one gives to any nameless member of a restaurant's staff. Clever girl, thought Julian. She had come here to check him out, his domestic set up – the real Julian. But how could she have... oh, never mind. He tried to enjoy the experience; she was obviously having fun. Sonia was, of course, in complete control. One knowing smile, a single stray word of familiarity from her or any sort of lingering eye contact and everything he had worked for would go up in a puff of spice infused smoke. She began another round of the restaurant floor (Julian knew he deserved one more). With her shoulders back, chest out and jaw set firm she strutted as slowly and magisterially as any young girl at the height of her powers (knowledge being the purest form of power) could strut. Julian gripped the worktop with both hands, so forcefully that all his fingers turned white. Through the black shiny leggings he could see her lean thigh and calf muscles alternately

250

tense and relax. Her bare heels slipped partially in and out of the shoes with each step she took. Sonia walked past Julian again, very close, almost brushing but not looking at him. He listened to her breathing: slow, deep and purring.

"Sorry about the mess," Stephanie called to her. "It's not finished yet. Come back in a few weeks and I promise, you'll love it."

"Yes, I have a feeling I will."

"So what about you? What do you do?"

"I'm in the entertainment business." Sonia swung round rapidly on one heel and walked briskly towards the door. She flashed a warm parting smile at the two women and left.

"Interesting young lady," said Allegra. "Such sexy clothes. You know, I'm pretty sure I've seen her before. Around this area, definitely. She's a local."

Stephanie's eyes widened. "You know her?"

"No, I've just seen her a couple of times, often with her boyfriend. He's much older than her. Big brute of a man." Stephanie nodded slowly and both ladies went back to their work.

Chapter 13

"What's this?" Stephanie's voice could be sweet at times, often melodious. This morning it just sounded irritated. Julian wasn't properly awake (he had been enjoying a very pleasant dream, the detail of which was now hazy) but he could tell Stephanie's question was rhetorical. It was blatantly obvious what 'it' was.

He squinted at it. "Uh, it's a business card, right?"

"Oh really?" Stephanie's voice was mocking. "Promises. Hottest new gentlemen's club. Quite an interesting *business*, wouldn't you say?" She had been going through his pockets. That bad habit would, without a doubt, only get worse after marriage.

"Where did you find that?"

"In one of your pockets. Where else? Just tell me Julian – where did you get it?"

"I can't remember. The streets are full of people handing out flyers, cards, adverts, whatnot. I probably just took it without realising."

"And if you *had* looked at it, you would have been shocked and given it straight back?"

"Yes. Obviously."

Stephanie seemed prepared to give him the benefit of the doubt. "As long as you're not planning a visit. Please don't become one of those… *gentlemen*."

"No, of course not."

Stephanie scrunched it up with both hands and threw it away. Julian followed its trajectory into the wastebasket with his eyes. "Why do so many men pay good money just to gawp at women's tits?" she said.

"I can't imagine."

Stephanie sighed. "Look, I don't want to go on about it, but this is something that makes me angry. It's exploitation. This is about young girls – some of them very young – taking their clothes off for money. How desperate do you need to be to do that?"

"You're right," Julian agreed, "It's shocking what some people do to make money. The lengths they go to."

Late in the afternoon, Julian managed to retrieve the card, half torn, from the wastepaper basket. It still retained some of its glossy, heavily embossed promise. He memorised the address (a familiar backstreet in Soho, just off Oxford Street) and tore it up into small pieces. In fact, its transformation into confetti had been perfectly timed: just at that moment he heard

Stephanie's key in the front door, followed by her tired footsteps. She had put in a full day at the restaurant. He had offered his services that morning; she had thanked him and told him that while appreciated, they were not essential. Apparently speed of production matters far more than aesthetic perfection as far as vegetable cubes are concerned.

"Hi Julian," she called to him, "what did you get up to today?"

"Administration. Just some essential paperwork." None of those words, taken individually, were untruths. He had administered to that festering, blood covered marble ashtray in his briefcase, a long neglected essential task. Several damp paper napkins had restored it to its shining original state, and it now rested on top of a small pile of books in the cabinet under his desk. It was anyone's guess what a wife-to-be might rummage through next. "Stephanie, are you staying in tonight?"

"Yes, I'm totally knackered. Why?"

"I've got a business meeting. I'm planning on taking a potential client out for dinner." He took a deep breath and went for it: "Do you want to join us?"

"No thanks, really, I'm much too tired. I wouldn't be much help."

As expected. He released the lungful of air. Julian was, in fact, no stranger to gentlemen's clubs. But for financial reasons he didn't visit them very often. Back in his university days he and Rob would slip into one unnoticed, on those quiet early weekday nights when entry was free of charge. They would buy one (overpriced) drink each and make it last as long as possible. A more recent trip – with a budget more suited to his new status in life – had cost Julian his monthly mortgage payment.

He chose clothing that was loose but stylish: light blue jeans and a very pale pink (practically white) shirt, unbuttoned to the top of his chest. Stephanie remarked on how nice it was to see him casually dressed instead of in those "boring old suits" and, waving at her, he skipped nimbly out of the door, closing it quietly.

Julian sat down in an almost empty carriage on the tube. He had to admit, he felt excited. Something special was bound to happen – but in reality, he had no idea what that might be. How could he manage the situation? Stephanie would expect him home at a reasonable time. Maybe he could book a hotel room and still make it back in time to appear as if he'd arrived hours earlier? Of course, everything depended on exactly what Sonia had in mind. He thought about yesterday at the restaurant: her slow strutting, that deep breathing. He had an overwhelming urge to get to Promises as fast as possible. Evidently, she had *something* in store for him.

The entrance was discreet: blacked out windows, the nude silhouette logo and name in italics as per the card. One rather average sized bouncer in a black suit spoke intermittently into a stick-like mouthpiece attached to his headset. An entirely non-threatening façade for the club, clearly intended to give a chap a last minute chance to think about what he was about to do before entering this den of iniquity. Julian took that chance. The bouncer made a point of looking everywhere but at him.

Automatically Julian pulled out his wallet. He knew it was adequately stuffed with twenties and fifties, but wanted to take another, final, look. He dreaded being caught short. A group of four men approached, early thirties or so, all dressed in pin stripe suits. They were chatting casually among themselves. With the slightest nod to the bouncer they were let in and immediately descended the stairs to the basement, jawing continuously. Regulars, thought Julian.

In a matter of a minute or so he too was sitting in that basement, sinking into an overly soft leather sofa. The place was dimly lit in a reddish hue, but bright lights shone onto a small, circular central stage, from which a single stainless steel pole rose upwards to its secure ceiling attachment. Beautiful, barely dressed young women strolled about in the distance, but for the time being none approached him. There was of course that few minutes' grace period in which a customer could order a drink and loosen his tie (Julian wasn't wearing one) before the attention started.

A smartly turned out waitress in her forties took his order. A large whiskey, neat, with a glass of tap water on the side. He sat back, looked around and waited for what was supposed to happen next. A very tall and shapely blonde girl sashayed up to him. He looked up at her; she beamed at him, he half smiled back and she took that as permission to sit next to him on the sofa, positioning herself so closely that their legs were in full contact.

"Hi!" she said joyfully, "and how are you, tonight, sir?"

"Hello. Fine, thanks," replied Julian, "You? Just had the first sip of my drink, actually."

"My name's Sapphire. What's yours?"

"Julian."

"Julian? Very nice. So English."

"So you're called Sapphire because of your eyes, right?" He pointed at them.

"Yes, ha ha, that's right. It's a good name for me, no?" There was a hint of central Europe about the accent. It was very mild, but he had always been very good with accents. "Julian, do you want me to dance for you?"

"Maybe a little later?" He smiled at her apologetically.

"Ohh," she pouted. Despite her great height she had the face of a very pretty little girl. "Later is too late. Maybe this will change your mind?" Both hands went up to her chest and she deftly unhooked part of her bra. The front sections fell away leaving only the straps. Two huge and impressively buoyant golden breasts stared at him. Sapphire grinned stupidly.

Julian tried holding her gaze but couldn't help looking down. He studied the uneven edges of her light brown nipples. "Actually I've come here to meet someone. Sonia. She works here. Do you know her?"

Sapphire covered herself up quickly. "*Sonia?* Yes, I know her. She works here."

"So, can you tell her I'm here?"

"Look, perhaps you should speak to the management about her, okay?" Sapphire got up and walked off. She didn't look back.

Julian sat back in the sofa again. The well dressed, fortyish woman (who wasn't a waitress but a greeter) was asking him if he wanted another drink. "Can you tell me if Sonia is here tonight?" he asked.

"Yes, she is. I can tell her you're here, if you want me to. Who shall I say–"

"Julian." She nodded and walked off. He looked at the performance in progress on the central stage. Two brunettes were dressed up in black leather. They were wearing flat topped military style caps – obviously in imitation of some sinister secret police force – and were looking upwards, seductively, from under the peak. Their cupless corsets (constructed to hoist surgically enhanced mammaries to chin level) and thigh length boots competed the look. One of them decided to up end herself and hang upside down from the steel pole, using only the sharp looking heels of her boots to hold herself in position. Pretty impressive, Julian thought, if only for its sheer athleticism.

The four men who had entered just before him were sitting tightly around one small table. They were talking to one another intensely, oblivious to what was going on around them and on the stage. Their table was overflowing with glasses, spirit and empty beer bottles. One dancer was plying her trade next to them, going through the motions of taking off and putting back on her skimpy, glittery dancewear, gyrating as the club's stereo system belted out one dance hit after another. She may as well have not been there.

The greeter returned. "Yes, Sonia will be free soon. She can meet you in one of our VIP rooms in about ten minutes. Why don't you go in and wait for her? Have a drink and relax."

"VIP room?" That meant expensive.

"Yes, let me explain how that works. It's basically three hundred pounds for each hour you're in there. Any drinks for yourself or the girl are extra. It's up to you how much you want to tip the girl but you don't have to pay her directly."

"Can I pay by credit card?" Julian realised his voice was hoarse.

"Yes, you can, but there is a fifteen percent surcharge on all card payments." Julian nodded. The greeter smiled warmly, and held up her arm. "It's this way."

The room itself was like a scaled down airport lounge for one person, only with much dimmer lighting. Julian sat on the expansive, smart looking grey leather sofa which was roomy enough for at least four people. It did suggest quite a range of possibilities for what went on in these places. The room was silent. Julian fidgeted and tapped his foot. The door opened, letting in some very bright light from the corridor outside. It shut again two seconds later. A young, smiling waitress, smartly dressed in a suit and frilly white collar, handed him a large, leather-bound drinks menu. "Just a bottle of champagne, please, two glasses. The cheapest one you've got."

"All our non-vintages are priced the same, four hundred pounds a bottle. How about the Moët?" Julian concurred. "Great, I'll bring that to you now in a bucket of ice along with two champagne flutes."

Which would arrive first, Sonia or the champagne? The large silver ice bucket was hauled in and Julian began sipping, very slowly, from one of the flutes. He wanted to relax but found himself sitting on the edge of the sofa, breathing far too fast. He crossed and uncrossed his legs in a futile attempt to make himself comfortable.

The door opened slowly and Sonia walked in. She closed the door gently and Julian immediately sat as far back in the sofa as he could. She was wearing something resembling a black bikini, but a closer look revealed that it was a G-string below and a harness-like contraption of straps and buckles on her chest. Her breasts were bare. Their neat, ovoid form seemed perfectly harmonised with her lean frame. On her feet were a pair of clear, colourless plastic high heeled open toe shoes. Stripper shoes.

She walked casually to the sofa and stood right in front of him. "Hello Julian." She almost smiled as her auburn bob shimmered. Julian took a deep breath, managed a smile and mumbled something. Sonia slipped off her heels and climbed on top of him, straddling his lap. She leaned backwards so her chest was at his eye level. The air conditioning in the room was quite strong, and her dark and surprisingly large nipples were very erect. They glared at him defiantly. He looked up at her mild brown eyes. She smiled sweetly. "Julian, let's start with the basics. The rules here are different. You're not allowed to touch me. I can touch you, but you can't lay a finger on me. Anywhere." Julian nodded firmly, making it clear he understood. "Well, I suppose that means we can begin."

She leaned in so that her face was right in front of his, the tips of their noses touching. She stuck her tongue out, positioned the tip on Julian's lower lip and then withdrew it, slowly, back into her mouth. She moved her head around, waggling it from side to side so her hair tickled his face. She was wearing some expensive, light floral perfume and her hair smelt very fresh, gloriously clean. "You know, Sapphire told me you were here," she said. "She didn't seem very happy. You could have got a dance from her, at least."

"Maybe. That reminds me of something. Sapphire, I mean. You're meant to use a stage name when you're stripping, not your real one. Everyone here knows you as Sonia."

She leaned back and looked him in the eye. "Ah, yes. You see, Sonia is my... how can I put this? It's my *working* name." Julian stared at her. "I also told you I was nineteen. Well, let's just say that's my working *age*."

"So... uh–"

She put her hands on his shoulders and rubbed them. "Shh," she said, smiling, "we're here to have fun." She began to rock backwards and forwards on his lap, slowly at first, then speeding things up a little. Julian's breathing and heart rate increased. Sensing this, she slowed down. "You know, it's amazing how close we are. To that final, long awaited union. I could whip off this G-string in a couple of seconds, and as for your zip... well, what do you think? I believe that other, much more important union – of our minds – happened long ago."

Julian took a very deep breath. "Okay. Let's go for it."

She stopped rocking and climbed off him. She sat down next to him and draped a slender bare arm across his shoulders. Crossing her legs, she tickled his ankle with her big toe and kissed him gently on the cheek. "Well it looks like we're all ready to go. Before I go and get the – uh, you know – protection, I just need to ask you something."

"Yes?"

"I went to visit Rob a couple of days ago. In hospital. He still hasn't come round."

"I see. I really hope he's making some progress, at least." Julian felt genuinely concerned.

"I don't think there's been any. But let me tell you something interesting, Julian."

"What?"

"Your friend was there. That detective guy. Toby."

"Oh really? You remember him?"

"From the nightclub, yep. Anyway, we were having a chat. About you."

Julian forced a smile. "Really?"

"Yes, *really*. He told me about Stephanie's restaurant. I can't wait to eat there." Was she sneering at him?

Julian sat up straight. "Okay Sonia, what is it you want to know?"

"I'll get to that. It's just that the conversation ended up getting pretty weird."

"In what way?"

"Toby is investigating Rob. Did you know that?"

263

"Yes, he did mention he was working on a case and that Rob was a suspect. I don't believe it myself."

"Nor do I," said Sonia. "What's weird is that it's a murder case. I mean, Rob? Murder?"

Julian cleared his throat. "Yes, crazy, isn't it?"

"Toby's theory is that he was short of cash and decided, out of the blue, to attack a wealthy old neighbour. He was so disturbed by what he had just done that he absent-mindedly walked into the road and almost killed himself."

Julian had almost forgotten that a near naked girl was sitting next to him. He was having to think extra fast. "Toby told me he'd spoken to Rob's housemates. Apparently he'd been acting completely out of sorts. Getting drunk almost every day."

"Toby thinks very highly of you, Julian. He'd never suspect you of anything. He knows what a hot shot financial wizard you are."

Julian coughed. "Well... ha, yes."

Sonia sat up very straight and uncrossed her legs. "So what I wanted to know was, why didn't you tell me you were with Rob when he got run over?"

"Because," Julian began – he sighed a long, weary sigh – "because I wanted to talk about other things. I would have told you everything about what had happened that day, eventually, if you'd really wanted to know. But that evening in the café, that was, well, about us." At last he was saying what he really meant.

"About... *us*?" Sonia looked completely blank. A teenager trying to fathom the bizarre workings of a

264

middle aged man's mind. "Okay," she said, "wait here. I'll be back." She got up and walked out of the door.

Julian sat back, once again, in the opulent leather sofa. It felt far too large for him. He noticed that the bottle of champagne was practically untouched. Sonia had taken a single sip from her glass: a lip gloss bow had been imprinted near the rim. Julian held his flute at angle and filled it right to the top in a sequence of shots, pausing long enough after each one for the foam to subside. He drank it off in two large gulps.

How long would Sonia be? Julian sat and waited. He became aware of an increasing sense of nervousness. Strips clubs were, after all, unpredictable places. High erotic glamour usually incurred great expense and, ultimately, disappointment. Okay, he'd give it half an hour from now. Let's see if Sonia returns.

The champagne was making his mouth dry. In spite of this he helped himself to another glass. He sipped this one more slowly, savouring its bitterness and the last of the effervescence before it went flat. Right, that was probably enough champagne for one night. He pressed the button for attention and a couple of minutes later the young waitress in the frilly collar reappeared. Julian ordered a bottle of still mineral water from her. When it arrived he unscrewed the cap and drank three quarters of it in large, continuous gulps.

Half an hour had passed. No sign of Sonia. He stood up, smoothed down his clothes and opened the door. He was no one's fool. Best just to call it a night, cut his losses and go home. He settled his (moderately eye-watering) bill and a few moments later found himself back outside

265

that discreet, subtly tempting entrance. The evening had become much cooler, as if high summer were about to take a week's break before resuming in earnest. Several small groups of men stood outside, all deciding whether to resist or simply give in and be led astray.

Julian felt like walking part of the way home. From the West End back to his house would have been a serious trek, but he simply intended to hail a taxi as soon as tiredness overtook him. He was curious to find out how far he'd get before his legs gave way. He breathed in a lungful of fresh, cool air and quickened his pace. He was determined to enjoy his walk.

Someone was walking behind him, roughly thirty feet further back. The footsteps were heavy and infrequent, suggesting a man of considerable height. Was he being followed? Julian stopped dead in his tracks to put that idea to the test. The sound that his ears had honed in on stopped too, a second or so later. What was going on? Julian had settled his bill in full. Had Sonia complained about his behaviour? Why would a bouncer be following him? No, don't be silly – they had far more important things to do than trail punters who had already been drained of their cash.

He turned into a narrow side street. That would sort things out once and for all – either the footsteps would stop or whoever was following him would have to reveal himself. He continued walking. He listened carefully; hearing nothing, he walked on at a more relaxed pace. If someone had been following him, Julian had managed to shake him off. Just to be sure, he turned round: no one. He sighed softly and continued moving forward. He chose the quickest route back onto the nearest decent sized road. It would be easy to hail a cab from there. Approaching the junction, he saw a couple of speeding black taxis with their reassuring orange light turned on. He quickened his pace for the last few metres.

A hand fell heavily on Julian's shoulder. He stopped breathing and froze. He felt incapable of moving any of his limbs. The hand tightened its grip. He waited for it to loosen but it didn't. He tried to turn round but realised he was rooted to the spot. The hand was pressing him down. What could he do? Before he could think of anything two large hands had gripped his upper arms and swung him round. Julian found himself staring up at that familiar, half smiling, almost shaved head on the enormous body. It was clad in the trademark long raincoat.

That guy you think is my pimp killed someone once. Julian took a deep breath. "Hello," he said. "It's... good to see you again. I was just talking to Son–" Raincoat man took a step back, bent down and drew his arm back as far as it would go. The fist was clenched. A second later it had been thrust into Julian's abdomen. He collapsed onto one knee, placing a hand on the pavement for support. He wondered when he'd be able to start breathing again. Thankfully he managed to take his first couple of breaths just before the large, this time slightly open hand whacked him across the face. He felt a searing pain in his cheek bone which soon turned into a dull, regular throb. And then he sensed the warm, thick flow of blood. Starting from his nose it trickled down over his closed lips onto his chin. Still on one knee, one hand still on the ground, Julian stuck the tip of his tongue out to taste the saltiness of his own plasma. Had that open handed punch broken his nose? Did it actually matter? It had always been aquiline, even from the most flattering angles. His looks (whatever they were) would be fairly intact.

Julian looked up. His assailant was looking down at him, a vaguely concerned expression on his face. Had Julian had enough? His attacker seemed to be debating that with himself. A moment later he kicked him: not viciously, but rather purposefully; a final, contemptuous shove with the foot that pushed Julian over. Raincoat man walked off, leaving Julian lying on the pavement on his side, a position he felt he could fall asleep in right there and then. An odd but interesting thought: physical pain wasn't so bad. Curiously liberating, actually. A refreshing change from the mental anguish of the last several days. Years, even.

Right – home. Better think about the best way to get back. Stephanie would (hopefully) be asleep, eliminating one major problem, at least for tonight. Julian realised a taxi was now out of the question. One look at his bloodied, broken face and any self-respecting cabbie would accelerate straight past him. He was just another brawling drunk tonight. He made sure to avoid his own reflection in any shop windows.

He got up. His legs were uninjured but he felt dizzy. Staggering, he walked forward a few feet. He stopped, held onto a metal railing and tried again. Yes, he would be okay. The walk home was about two hours. (He had done it before as a student, when he'd been short of the cab fare but unwilling to sit with people more inebriated than himself on a night bus). He joined the main road. Couples – decent young people who had just had a civilised night out – stared at him. They quickly looked away when he stared back. He felt small. People like that had no idea what he had been through. If only he could tell them his story. Would they understand?

Hunching slightly – his guts were still very sore – he put one foot in front of the other and walked. Garish neon lit bars and chain restaurants turned into upmarket designer shops, which themselves gave way to their poor cousins, the discount chains. Then came the vast regency houses of the inner suburbs, followed by the dark (almost black at this time) green hue of the sprawling heath and finally his smiling front door, welcoming the bloodied warrior home.

He entered the kitchen. A large, sticky-backed yellow notepaper with a handwritten message was stuck to a cupboard. He pulled it off.

Julian –
Hope you had a fun (and of course profitable) evening with your client. Was planning a quiet night in but then felt I had to go out and do something. Allegra wanted to hit the town and I couldn't resist. After all, it's been ages since we did anything fun. So, it's going to be a late one tonight – see you tomorrow morning!
Steph x

He read and reread it, staring at it for so long that it was as if he wanted some of his blood to drip onto it.

But by now it had dried all over his face. No, those cherrywood floors he'd paid for would remain unsullied by his body tissues. He trudged up the stairs. There seemed to be nowhere else to go other than his study. He sat down and opened the cupboard under the desk. He put the marble ashtray to one side, took out the two large books underneath it and put them on the desk. Two hefty hardbacks with something nestling in between them. Something made of cloth. He prised the books apart and fished it out. It was his yarmulke, slightly creased but otherwise pristine. He studied the fine silver embroidery on the blue background. He folded it neatly and placed it on the edge of the desk.

Julian picked up the book on top. *Crime and Punishment.* Putting it aside, he looked at the even weightier volume underneath. *Elevator Systems Design: Concepts and Theory.* He opened the heavy front cover and his own handwriting from years ago informed him that this book was the property of J. Kiel. He skipped past the first twenty or so pages – the copious forewords, prefaces and introduction – and started reading at chapter one.

19427166R00162